Dear Reader,

As a card-carrying member of Workaholics Anonymous, I completely identify with Finn O'Roarke. He brews beer for a living and I write stories, but we're from the same tribe. We get a whole lot accomplished, but we can't seem to locate the off switch.

Because of that, I loved hauling Finn from his microbrewery in Seattle to his cowboy roots in Wyoming so he could rediscover the simple joys of ranch life and maybe even allow himself to fall in love. The core values he learned as a foster kid at Thunder Mountain Ranch might be the very things that save him from himself.

And for those of you who loved my Sons of Chance series, I have a treat for you in this book. You'll get to revisit the Last Chance Ranch and catch up with some of your old friends. I promised that the Thunder Mountain Brotherhood series would intersect with the Sons of Chance series here and there, and this is one of those times!

So grab a cool drink and a shady spot because I have plenty to tell you and you won't want to miss a single thing. You especially won't want to miss the moment when Finn realizes it's time to cowboy up!

Your devoted storyteller,

Vicki Lewis Thompson

Vicki Lewis Thompson

Rolling Like Thunder

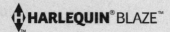

Recycling programs
for this product may
not exist in your area.

ISBN-13: 978-0-373-79859-9

Rolling Like Thunder

Copyright © 2015 by Vicki Lewis Thompson

Printed in U.S.A.

A passion for travel has taken *New York Times* bestselling author **Vicki Lewis Thompson** to Europe, Great Britain, the Greek isles, Australia and New Zealand. She's visited most of North America and has her eye on South America's rainforests. Africa, India and China beckon. But her first love is her home state of Arizona, with its deserts, mountains, sunsets and—last but not least—cowboys! The wide-open spaces and heroes on horseback influence everything she writes. Connect with her at vickilewisthompson.com, facebook.com/vickilewisthompson and twitter.com/vickilthompson.

Books by Vicki Lewis Thompson

HARLEQUIN BLAZE

Sons of Chance

Should've Been a Cowboy
Cowboy Up
Cowboys Like Us
Long Road Home
Lead Me Home
Feels Like Home
I Cross My Heart
Wild at Heart
The Heart Won't Lie
Cowboys & Angels
Riding High
Riding Hard
Riding Home
A Last Chance Christmas

Thunder Mountain Brotherhood

Midnight Thunder
Thunderstruck

To get the inside scoop on Harlequin Blaze and its talented writers, be sure to check out blazeauthors.com.

All backlist available in ebook format.

Visit the Author Profile page at Harlequin.com for more titles.

To Wendy Delaney, fellow author and awesome Seattle friend. If O'Roarke's Brewhouse existed, we'd meet there for a drink!

1

FINN O'ROARKE SCANNED the boarding area for the ump-teenth time. First class was already on the plane and still no Chelsea. He would have gladly picked her up instead of meeting her here, but they hadn't been able to agree on timing. He preferred early and she liked to cut it close.

Too damned close. Good thing he didn't fly with her on a regular basis, because this kind of thing would drive him…ah! There she was. He exhaled and promised him-self not to say a word. She was doing him a favor by making this trip.

With a roller bag behind her and a laptop case over her shoulder, she walked toward the boarding area with her typical "I have the world by the tail" stride. She wasn't tall but she dressed tall—skinny black jeans, high-heeled sandals and a multicolored tunic belted around her hips. Her light blond hair, recently streaked with lavender, swayed gently with each confident step.

As she came closer, she surveyed the crowd waiting near the Jetway and her brown eyes widened when she spotted him. She hurried over. "Holy smokes, you're dressed like a cowboy! I did not expect that."

At one time Finn would have been annoyed. But after

owning a Seattle microbrewery and tavern for nearly five years, he didn't think of himself as a cowboy anymore. He couldn't very well expect her to think of him that way, either.

But they'd be spending time at the Last Chance Ranch in Jackson Hole this weekend. Finn had never seen it, but he'd heard plenty of stories. The Chance family was royalty in Wyoming.

So he'd hauled out his dove-gray Stetson, his yoked Western shirts, his Wranglers and his black boots. He gazed at Chelsea and shrugged. "We're making our presentation to ranch people. It seemed like a good idea."

"Should I have done that, too? If so, I'm screwed. I have these sandals and gym shoes. That's it."

"No worries, Chels. You'll be fine." He thought she looked more than fine. He'd known from the moment they'd met in a coffee shop five years ago that she was too cool and stylish for him.

But meeting her had been a gift. She was a PR and marketing whiz. After listening to his plan for a microbrewery and tavern in downtown Seattle, she'd suggested a Kickstarter crowdfunding campaign to renovate an old building slated for demolition. Then she'd offered to help him for a percentage. He'd saved the building and launched O'Roarke's Brewhouse thanks to Chelsea Trask.

This trip would put him even more in her debt. His foster parents, Herb and Rosie Padgett, were in financial trouble and could lose the ranch where Finn and many other homeless boys had found refuge. A group of them were trying to save it, and because Chelsea knew Finn's background and admired the Padgetts, she'd agreed to help him once again.

Thanks to Chelsea, a Kickstarter campaign had been launched in June for Thunder Mountain Academy, a residential equine education program geared toward teens. But the September 1 deadline for donations was less than two weeks away and they were thousands shy of the goal. Everybody connected with it, including Finn, had begun to panic.

This weekend was make-or-break time. Cade Gallagher, once a foster boy and one of Finn's best friends, had recently discovered he was a Chance cousin. Because of that family tie, Finn and Chelsea had been invited to pitch the concept to potential TMA backers at a gathering hosted by the Chances. Chelsea was the pro, so she'd run the event, but Finn would also talk about the debt he owed Thunder Mountain Ranch.

As the first economy-class group was called to board the plane, Chelsea gave Finn another once-over. "It's probably good that you're all decked out like that."

"I'm glad you approve." He decided not to let the "all decked out" comment bother him, either. Coming from Chelsea, that was a relatively mild dig. When she was wound up, she could really turn on the snark. She'd been irritated with him for months, which made working together on this project somewhat awkward.

Apparently she'd expected them to get together after his divorce from Alison last year, but she, of all people, should have realized that he was married to his business, which was why Alison had left. Yeah, he'd had his share of hot dreams starring Chelsea, but he had no intention of turning them into reality.

Guaranteed if they got together, it'd disrupt his careful routine right when he needed to concentrate all his energy on keeping the microbrewery solvent. The divorce had been expensive. Besides, he'd proved himself incapable of running a business and maintaining a relationship. He'd told her that when he'd turned down her dinner invitation, but she hadn't taken it well.

Because they'd bought their plane tickets late, they'd be in the last group to board, so she had time to study him. "I remember the hat and boots from when we did the photo shoot for the Men of Thunder Mountain calendar, but that was a deliberate beefcake shirtless shot. This is more subtle, but effective."

"Effective for what?" He'd suffered through the photo session last month because some genius had decided Thunder Mountain Academy needed a calendar as a giveaway to backers. Chelsea had volunteered to take his picture rather than having him waste time flying to Wyoming.

"Image." She gave him another assessing glance. "While my PowerPoint presentation is running, you can stand there looking like a guy who can ride and rope with the best of them—all the things they plan to teach students at Thunder Mountain Academy."

Okay, he couldn't let that go. "As it happens, I *can* ride and rope. Maybe not with the best of them anymore because I'm out of practice, but I'd be decent."

"I'm sure you would." Her gaze warmed briefly before she broke eye contact. "Hey, that's us." She waved her boarding pass. "Time to rock and roll."

"Right." She'd captured his attention so completely that he'd missed the announcement. Perfect example of how she distracted him. Adjusting the shoulder strap of his laptop case and grasping the handle of his wheeled bag, he followed her.

Chelsea could sure stir him up. Now he had the adolescent urge to actually do some riding and roping on this trip just to prove to her that he could. Not at the Last Chance, of course, but they'd planned to drive over to

Thunder Mountain Ranch for a few days afterward so she could look over the setup for TMA.

After all the work she'd put into nurturing the idea and giving advice—all gratis—she deserved to see the ranch and meet his foster parents. They were eager to meet her, too. He wondered if she rode. He'd never asked.

As they entered the plane a blonde flight attendant smiled at him. "Great hat."

"Thank you, ma'am." He was out of the habit of using *ma'am*, but he'd unconsciously lapsed into it.

"I'd be glad to store it up front for you."

"That would be great." He took it off and handed it to her.

"My pleasure." She gave him another brilliant smile. "I'll take good care of it."

"I surely appreciate that." Yep. He was back to talking like a cowboy.

By the time he caught up with Chelsea, she was struggling to get her roller bag into the overhead compartment, so he helped her. She muttered her thanks and he slid his own in next to it before taking his seat.

The plane was configured with two seats on one side of the aisle and three on the other, and Chelsea had managed to snag the two-seat side when she'd made their reservations. She'd requested the window, which was fine with him because he preferred the aisle.

Once they were buckled in, she turned to him. "'Thank you, ma'am'?"

"I swear it's the hat. I put it on and my words come out different."

"You wore it for the photo shoot and I didn't notice you calling me ma'am."

He laughed. "That's because you were torturing me

by making me hold a beer keg on my bare shoulder for hours on end."

"Minutes, O'Roarke. Mere minutes. You were such a baby about that shoot."

"It was embarrassing, posing shirtless and knowing come April I'll be tacked up on someone's wall."

"That reminds me...I brought calendars."

He groaned. "I was afraid you would."

"It's a sales tool. Of course I had to bring them. You haven't seen the final product, have you?" She pulled her laptop case out from under the seat in front of her.

"No, and I don't want to see it now."

"You need to look at it. Don't forget, the Chance brothers volunteered, so this will give you a mental picture of each one before we get there." She unzipped her case and pulled out a calendar.

There was his buddy Cade on the front, manly and shirtless as he leaned against the hitching post with a rope coiled over one shoulder. "I don't need that kind of mental picture of the Chance brothers, thank you very much."

"The pictures aren't all like that." She flipped through the calendar. "See? Here's Jack Chance, fully dressed, sitting on his horse Bandit. He looks part Native American, don't you think?"

"I guess." Finn had to admit that seeing the men in advance would help him remember their names when he met them.

"And here's Nick Chance, Dominique's husband. My picture of you is okay, but I'm glad Dominique was available to take the bulk of the shots because she's such an amazing photographer. And obviously in love with Nick."

Finn looked at the close-up of a smiling cowboy with dark hair and green eyes. His hat was shoved back, which

made him seem friendly, as if he'd be a good guy to share
a beer with. "You're right. This helps. Where's Gabe?"

"Here." Chelsea flipped to a picture of a sandy-haired
man with a mustache. "Dominique said she had to heckle
him to get him to unsnap his shirt but he finally did it."

"At least he was allowed to wear a shirt." Finn gazed
at the image of Gabe leading a brown-and-white Paint
out of the barn. "Some of us weren't so lucky."

"Hey, what have you got there?" The flight attendant
paused next to his seat. "Oh, let me see!"

Before Finn could protest, Chelsea handed it to her.

"I love this! Can I hold on to it until after takeoff? I'll
bring it back."

"Sure," Chelsea said. "Take your time."

As the flight attendant walked toward the front of
the plane, Finn turned to glare at Chelsea. "Now you've
done it."

"You were the one charming her with your hat and
your 'thank you, ma'am' routine."

"I was just trying to be polite, but now she's—"

"A potential backer for Thunder Mountain Academy.
Obviously your cowboy persona will be an asset this
weekend. It never occurred to me that you should dress
and act the part, although it should have, so props to you.
Brilliant PR move."

"I wasn't thinking of it as a PR move." In some ways
it had been a protective one. When a guy ended up in a
foster home with no relatives to call his own, he tried to
put his best foot forward whenever possible. Finn also
owned a three-piece suit, but he was Wyoming born and
knew that a suit wouldn't impress the Chance family
nearly as much as a nice hat and polished boots.

"It's a good look for you, Finn. You should dress like
this more often."

He shook his head.

"Why not?"

"Because I refuse to be one of those guys who wears the clothes because he thinks they look cool but who's never sat a horse or mucked out a stall." He wished to hell the flight attendant didn't have that calendar. Knowing they'd be mailed out to people he'd never met and probably never would meet was one thing. This was completely different.

"But you have ridden and…what was that other thing?"

"Mucked out a stall. Cleaned it out, in other words."

She studied him. "I can picture you doing that, especially now that I've seen you in this outfit. But I hope you don't wear that gorgeous gray hat to muck out a stall."

"No, that's my dress hat. Herb keeps some old straw ones for everyday chores."

"Oh, right. You were wearing something like that when all of you were at the ranch in June and you Skyped me about Kickstarter ideas. FYI, the gray felt is a vast improvement over that battered straw thing."

"Thanks."

"What? No 'thank you, ma'am'?"

He decided to lay it on thick. Served her right. He gave her his most winning smile and his deepest drawl. "Thank you, ma'am."

She stared at him for a full three seconds. Then she swallowed and looked away. "You're welcome."

Uh-oh. He'd meant it sarcastically, but apparently it hadn't affected her that way. Unless he was mistaken, he'd just turned her on. And that could present a problem.

Hell, who was he kidding? They'd always had a problem. From that first day in the coffee shop he'd been fascinated by her creativity and zest for life. He loved watching her talk and hearing her laugh. Her mouth was perfect and her skin was impossibly soft, not that he allowed himself to touch it except by accident.

The thought of interacting with her on a personal level as well as a business one scared the crap out of him. If he once gave in and took her to bed, he'd never get a damned thing done. He'd made sure to focus solely on the business angle of their relationship, at least when he was awake. He couldn't control his dreams.

Then he'd met Alison. Quiet and methodical, she'd been the complete opposite of Chelsea. Alison had made it clear that she wanted him and had pushed for a commitment. He'd had some stupid idea that she was the kind of steady, safe woman he needed in his life.

Marrying her, especially so quickly, had been a huge mistake. She hadn't absorbed all his attention, but she hadn't held his interest, either. She'd been understandably upset by his total concentration on his business. He felt damned guilty about that marriage.

And he'd promised himself not to repeat his mistake. These days he only allowed two things to occupy his time: O'Roarke's Brewhouse and his foster parents' financial crisis. Making sure they weren't forced to sell out was his priority this week. As the plane lifted into the air, he renewed his vow that Thunder Mountain Ranch would stay in the family.

CHELSEA GAZED AT white clouds piled up like whipped cream outside the window. And speaking of whipped cream, she wouldn't mind being alone with a naked Finn and a can of the stuff. Their trip was minutes old and she was already in trouble.

His lustrous dark hair and startling blue eyes had caught her attention immediately when they'd met in that coffee shop five years ago. His body was nothing to sneeze at, either. When he'd first arrived in Seattle he'd had a tan, but that had gradually faded. His sex appeal hadn't faded one tiny bit, though. Finn O'Roarke was hot.

Although they'd had chemistry from the beginning, he'd made it clear that he wasn't interested in anything more than friendship and a business relationship. Disappointing, but she'd learned to live with it. At least she'd been able to see him often, and she'd noted with satisfaction that he spent all his time on work and didn't date.

Then the rat had showed up with Alison and in practically no time at all they'd been married. Chelsea had hated that with a purple passion, and when the marriage had predictably broken up, she'd decided enough was enough. She'd waited a decent interval and then she'd asked him out. He'd turned her down.

That was so unfair. Just because Alison had complained about his lack of attention didn't mean she would. She understood the constraints on his time and she had her share of those, too.

But he'd retreated into his anal-retentive shell and wasn't coming out. She longed to give him up as a lost cause, but he sent her checks every month and that guaranteed she couldn't forget him. Then this situation with his foster parents had brought them back together and, once again, she was into him.

Worse yet, he'd added a new level of hotness with his cowboy shtick. She hadn't realized she was susceptible to cowboys. Or maybe it was only Cowboy Finn who made her heart beat faster. She'd find that out after being surrounded by a bunch of them for the next few days.

Last month her first big challenge had presented itself. Logically she'd been the one to handle his calendar shoot and she'd counted on her irritation with his behavior to see her through. It hadn't.

She'd mostly blamed the shirtless part for her overheated state. Finn's hair was the kind a woman itched to run her fingers through. Turned out he had a sprinkling of that same tantalizing dark hair on his rather impressive chest and it also formed a narrow path that led to the low-slung waistband of his jeans.

The shoot had taken longer than necessary because she'd spent far too much time wondering what he kept hidden behind that denim fly. She suspected he had a package worth bragging about, but Finn wasn't the bragging type. Of course that made him all the more tempting. After photographing him posing shirtless and wearing the Stetson, jeans and boots, she'd hurried home to commune with her vibrator.

Sadly that was the extent of her sex life lately. After his quickie marriage, she'd indulged in a couple of affairs that had gone nowhere. The torch still burned for Finn despite all her efforts. She'd protected herself by being cool and sarcastic in his presence—until a moment ago when he'd given her that high-wattage smile and a sensuous "thank you, ma'am."

A man as beautiful as Finn shouldn't be allowed to talk like that. He also shouldn't wear yoked shirts that made his shoulders seem a mile wide and jeans that cradled the sexiest buns in Seattle. But he had no idea that he was a walking sexual fantasy. The flight attendant had fallen all over herself sending "I'm available" signals and he hadn't seemed to notice. Now that she had the calendar, Finn might discover a phone number tucked into his hatband.

But he was Chelsea's for the next week, or as close to being hers as she'd ever experienced. He'd also left his precious business in the hands of his assistant, Brad.

With luck he might learn that he wasn't so damned in-dispensable, after all.

But she couldn't allow thoughts about sexy Finn to distract her from her first order of business—wooing TMA backers during the presentation at the Last Chance Ranch. She'd continued to work on the PowerPoint until after midnight, which had caused her to oversleep. Now that the plane was at cruising altitude, she could take another look at it.

Finn, she noticed, was already engrossed in his Excel file. She'd retrieved her laptop and had balanced it on her fold-down tray when the flight attendant showed up with the calendar.

All her attention was on Finn, who remained en-grossed in his spreadsheets. "You're Mr. April, aren't you?"

His head snapped up and he flushed as he stared at her in dismay. "Uh, yeah."

"Gorgeous."

He swallowed. "It was…we needed…"

"What's the deal with Thunder Mountain Academy?"

"It's this…this—"

"A residential equine program for sixteen-to-eighteen-year-olds," Chelsea said. "It'll be a fabulous opportunity for kids who think they might want to build a career around horses. They'll learn horse training and equine health care along with the daily maintenance required. In addition, we have a master saddle maker who'll teach them the basics of that art."

The flight attendant blinked. "Sounds great, but I don't have any kids. Can I just buy the calendar?"

"It's offered as a premium if you pledge a certain amount to the academy's Kickstarter fund." Chelsea pulled out a card with website information on it. "Here's where you can do that. It's all spelled out on the site."

"Thanks." She took the card and reluctantly handed back the calendar. "Maybe some of my girlfriends will want to go together on it." She glanced down at Finn. "I'm a beer drinker, too."

He cleared his throat. "Good."

"Don't forget your hat when you leave the plane."

"I won't."

"'Bye, now." She fluttered her fingers at him and headed back to the front of the plane.

"Good Lord." Finn sank back against the seat and took several deep breaths. "Thanks for telling her about TMA. My mind went blank."

"I noticed."

"Obviously, I'm not prepared for the effect that calendar is liable to have."

"It's not just the calendar." Chelsea gazed at him. "So how long since you've dressed like a cowboy?"

"About five years. Basically since I moved to Seattle. Why?"

"Oh, it's just that some guys get more appealing as the years go by and some get less. You might be in the first category."

He laughed and shook his head. "No. It's the calendar. I just have to brace myself for the reaction to it from now on."

"If you say so." She tucked the calendar back in her laptop case. Then she dug around for her earbuds because she wanted to hear the background music she'd chosen to accompany her PowerPoint, as well as the sound for the accompanying videos. At last she cued it up on the screen and put in the earbuds. "Back to work."

Finn tapped her on the shoulder and she pulled out an earbud. "What?"

"Can I listen, too?"

"Okay." Sharing the earbuds meant leaning close to each other, but she wouldn't mind getting his input even if it meant putting up with the warmth of his body, the delicious scent of his aftershave and the sound of his breathing.

Once they were huddled together, she started the PowerPoint. Focusing on it with him so close wasn't easy, but it was a good test of whether the presentation was any good. She'd opened with stirring music and the TMA logo: a horseshoe with the letters at the top created to resemble snowy mountain peaks. Next was a slide of the snowcapped Big Horn Mountain range with her shout line: Thunder Mountain Academy—Built on a Foundation of Caring.

Rosie had sent her some old photos of the ranch during its years as a foster-care facility and Chelsea had created a montage along with some explanatory text. Finn as a teenager appeared in several of the pictures. She heard his breath catch as he watched.

She'd introduced the next segment with the title "A New Era Dawns" and a brief explanation of the program. Then she'd included videos of Lexi, Cade's girlfriend, giving riding lessons, plus one of Cade schooling a horse. Herb, a retired veterinarian, was shown delivering a foal. Ben Radcliffe would teach saddle making, and he'd sent some beautiful photos of his work. The academic benefits of the program were outlined, and then Rosie appeared in shots of an outdoor feast around a large campfire.

A brief video tour of the ranch house, the barn and the four log cabins where the students would live rounded out the presentation. It ended with a picture of Rosie,

Herb, Cade, Lexi and Ben all wearing T-shirts bearing the TMA logo as they stood smiling in front of the ranch house. The last slide was once again set against the Big Horn range and carried the slogan "Thunder Mountain Academy. Fostering respectful stewardship of our equine friends through experience and education."

The music swelled to a crescendo and faded as the image on the screen slowly disappeared. Chelsea thought it was pretty good. Not perfect, but then she was never completely satisfied with her work.

Beside her, Finn took a deep breath as he removed his earbud. "That was spectacular."

"Oh, I'm not so sure it's spectacular, but—"

"No, Chels, it's spectacular." He settled his intense blue gaze on her. "And you're not charging us a dime, either. I don't know how I'll ever be able to thank you."

As she looked into his eyes she could think of several ways, but he wouldn't want to hear them. "Aren't we supposed to meet the Chance family at a saloon called the Spirits and Spurs tonight?"

"That's the plan."

"Then once we get there, you can buy me a drink." It wasn't what she really wanted from him, but for now it would have to do.

2

FINN WOULD HAVE liked to watch the presentation again, but Chelsea wanted to polish it some more. She spent the rest of the trip, including the layover in Salt Lake City, tweaking it. And she accused *him* of being anal.

After they landed in Jackson, they picked up the gray SUV she'd reserved and he drove to the little town of Shoshone while she continued to play with the Power-Point file.

"You're missing the scenery."

"That's okay." She didn't look up from the screen. "I'll see it on the way back."

"Surely it's done by now."

"Mostly, but every time I look at it I see one more thing I want to fix. The presentation tomorrow is super important."

"I'm well aware of that, but the version I saw on the plane should do the trick."

"It's way better now." Her fingers flew over the keyboard of her laptop. "There. That font pops more than the other one."

"There's such a thing as working a project to death, you know."

She glanced up. "Did you really say that? You, a card-carrying member of Perfectionists Anonymous?"

"I'm beginning to think you founded the club. I don't remember you fiddling this much with the O'Roarke's Brewhouse PowerPoint."

"That's because I worked on it in the middle of the night and you weren't there. How would you feel if something this important was riding on your expertise?"

He contemplated that. "I see what you mean."

"Thank you." There was triumph in her voice. "If you'd been the one responsible for this very important PowerPoint, you would have made me drive while you worked on it."

"Well, you're going to have to stop because there's the Bunk and Grub up ahead. We don't have much time to check in before we head over to meet the Chance family at the saloon."

She turned off her laptop and tucked it into her carrying case. "Looks just like the picture on the website, a cute little Victorian. With a name like the Bunk and Grub, you'd think it would be more rustic."

"The Spirits and Spurs is rustic. We passed it on the way here."

"Is it close?"

"A couple of blocks. We could walk it." Then he thought of her high-heeled sandals. "Or not. I forgot about your shoes."

"If I can take the hills of Seattle in these I can certainly walk a couple of blocks on flat ground." She glanced down at her outfit. "But are you sure I'll be okay wearing this? Not that I have anything more Western and rustic to change into."

"Chels, you'd look great in a feed sack." He wondered

if he should have said that. But it was true. She had an instinctive sense of style.

"Unfortunately, I didn't bring a feed sack. I don't even know what they look like, but I'm sure they're rustic. Being a cowboy and all, you probably know all about them."

He laughed. "I do. Listen, whatever you brought will be fine, unless you decide to go riding while we're at Thunder Mountain. Then maybe we should pick up a couple of things in Sheridan. Or you might be able to borrow a pair of boots from Rosie or Lexi, depending on sizes."

"Could we do that? Go riding?"

"That's up to you. Ever been on a horse?"

"I have, but it's been…jeez, fifteen years. I took some lessons. And I rode English."

"Huh. I didn't know that." He pulled into the parking lot beside the Bunk and Grub and shut off the engine.

"I'll bet there's a lot you don't know about me."

"Probably so." He met her gaze. He'd deliberately avoided finding out too much for fear it would only create more connection between them. Like the riding thing. Although she hadn't kept it up, at one time experiencing the world on horseback had appealed to her.

"If it isn't too much trouble, I'd love to go riding when we get to Thunder Mountain. I'll be rusty, but I think it would be fun to get on a horse again. If the horse is gentle, I should be fine wearing my gym shoes."

"Then I'll take you." He broke eye contact and reached for the door handle. "There's a Forest Service road through the trees. You'll like it." And damned if it didn't sound like a romantic thing to do.

"I'm sure I will." She opened her door and climbed out.

The walkway around to the front door of the B and B

was a series of stepping stones set in gravel, so Finn offered to carry both suitcases and Chelsea took their laptop shoulder bags. As he followed her up the steps to a front porch decorated with white wicker furniture and floral cushions, his mind was still on that ride along the Forest Service road.

He hadn't thought much about the second part of this trip, but now that he knew she had some riding experience, he wanted to show her everything—the little clearing where he, Cade and Damon had performed their blood-brother ceremony, the stream where the three of them used to camp when they were older, and the slope they'd cleared of trees so they could use it as a toboggan run in the winter.

She'd like Cade and Damon. Finn was looking forward to seeing them again. So much had changed since he'd been there in June. Cade and Lexi had gotten back together, although still no word on a wedding. Damon had moved back to Sheridan to be with Philomena, the carpenter who'd worked with him on a fourth cabin for TMA last month.

Finn had been back to the ranch a few times since moving to Seattle, but he'd always traveled alone. This would be the first time he'd ever taken someone there. Maybe it was fitting that Chelsea should be the one. She'd helped him make the transition to Seattle and now she'd be able to see where he'd come from. For her, at least, the picture would be complete.

But he had huge gaps in his knowledge of her. He didn't feel good about that. When it came to Chelsea, he'd been a coward. He should be able to get to know the woman's background without forming an inseparable bond. As he walked through the front door of the

Bunk and Grub, he decided to use this weekend to learn more about her.

The reception area and an adjacent parlor matched the exterior. Antique furniture and gilt-framed mirrors reminded Finn of the pictures his grandfather had showed him of his great-grandparents' house. Vases of fresh flowers were everywhere.

A middle-aged woman with blond hair rose from behind an antique desk and came forward when they walked in. "You must be Finn and Chelsea."

"We are." Chelsea held out her hand. "And you must be Pam Mulholland. I recognize you from your picture on the website."

"I'm Pam." She took Chelsea's hand in both of hers. "And I'm so excited about Thunder Mountain Academy. I've been talking to everyone I know. You should have a good crowd at the Last Chance tomorrow afternoon."

"My goodness, thank you!"

"The project sounds amazing." She squeezed Chelsea's hand and released it. "And, Finn, I'm delighted to meet you."

"Same here, ma'am." He touched the brim of his hat. "I also want to thank you for getting the word out about tomorrow. Thunder Mountain means a great deal to a lot of people, me included."

"I'm sure it does. When Cade visited last month he kept us all entertained with stories about the days when you boys lived there."

He smiled. "Don't believe everything you hear."

"So you weren't the one who glued the toilet seats shut and put salt in the sugar bowl?"

"Uh, well…" He made a mental note to have a talk with his old buddy Cade.

Pam laughed. "You wouldn't be normal kids if you

hadn't pulled a few pranks. According to Sarah, the Chance boys—"

A grandfather clock in the parlor chimed, interrupting her. "Whoops. Time to get moving." She hurried behind the desk and grabbed two sets of keys from a board on the wall. "The bigger one opens the front door when I'm not here and the smaller one's a room key. You can both sign the register later. You two are my only guests this weekend, so we can be more informal."

"That sounds nice," Chelsea said.

"I won't abandon all the protocol, but I've dispensed with our usual happy hour for obvious reasons. You'll be at Spirits and Spurs tonight and at the ranch for dinner tomorrow. We can see about Sunday night's happy hour if you end up hanging around here."

"We might," Finn said. "It's a great house."

"Thank you." Pam looked pleased. "I love it. Oh, and if you should need anything while you're here, dial zero from the phone in your room. It'll connect to me, or if I'm not here, it goes to the housekeeper's room. Yvonne will take care of you. Are you walking over to Spirits and Spurs or driving?"

"Walking," Chelsea said without hesitation.

"Then I'll walk with you. Come on down whenever you're ready and we'll head over. Everyone's so eager to meet you." Pam glanced at Finn. "Josie has the beer you shipped chilling even as we speak. Nice touch."

Chelsea swung around to gaze at him. "You sent beer? What a great idea."

"Testing the market."

"Smart." She glanced at the number attached to her set of keys. "Which way is Room Three?"

"Up the stairs and to your left." She handed Finn the

other key. "You're in Four, right next to her. They're my two favorites."

Finn took the key with a smile. "Much obliged, ma'am." From the corner of his eye he caught Chelsea's smirk. But he was in cowboy country now. He'd felt it the minute they'd landed in Jackson, and the Western atmosphere brought back all his cowboy manners. He hefted both suitcases and started toward the stairs.

"Oh, and in case I get caught up in the dancing and forget to mention it," Pam said, "breakfast is at eight. Just follow your nose to the coffee and you'll find the breakfast room."

"Dancing?" Finn paused to glance back at her.

"At the Spirits and Spurs. There's a live band and a dance floor. You and Chelsea will have to try it out."

"Definitely," Chelsea called over her shoulder as she started up the stairs. "Right, Finn?"

"Right." Good Lord, would he really have to do that? He followed her up the stairs and down the carpeted hallway. "I'm not much of a dancer," he said quietly as he set her suitcase by her door.

"Me, either."

"Really? Or are you just saying that to make me feel better?"

"No, really." She unlocked the door and turned to face him. "I hung out with the brainy kids. We considered ourselves too cool to go to dances, so I never really learned how. I sort of regret it now."

"That's surprising. I pictured you being into the whole social thing, maybe even the homecoming queen."

She burst out laughing. "Oh, Finn, you have a lot to learn about me. You can start tonight as you steer me awkwardly around the dance floor."

"We're not actually going to do it, are we?" He stared at her in horror.

"Of course we are. Pam's remark tells me that these folks love their dancing. It's like when you're in a country where you don't speak the language. The locals appreciate it if you at least give it a try. Sitting there like bumps on a log would be a mistake. We should dance, even if we're bad at it. It'll be excellent PR."

"It'll be a disaster."

"No, it won't." She gazed up at him. "It'll do us both good. We've established that we're both perfectionists and we probably carry that to an extreme."

"Speak for yourself."

"I'm speaking for both of us. Let's see if we can tolerate dancing badly."

He groaned.

"Man up, O'Roarke. Have a few beers. Cut loose. I know you have it in you after hearing about the toilet seats and the sugar-to-salt routine."

"Okay, but you'll be sorry. You're wearing sandals, don't forget, and I'm wearing boots. Don't blame me if you're limping by the end of the night."

"I won't blame you, but I might ask you to give me a foot rub."

His breath caught.

"See you in five minutes, cowboy." Grabbing her suitcase, she handed him his laptop, ducked inside her door and closed it in his face.

He stared at the closed door for several seconds. *A foot rub.* She was taunting him, which wasn't very nice of her, all things considered. But, God, how he loved it.

TWENTY MINUTES LATER when Chelsea walked into the Spirits and Spurs, she recognized immediately that this was the real deal. She'd seen places that gave the appearance of being historic frontier watering holes, but this saloon had earned its ambience the old-fashioned way through years of serving drinks to thirsty cowhands.

The tables were scarred but sturdy, while the polished wooden bar, complete with beveled mirror behind it and plenty of shelves and brass fittings, was a thing to behold. Finn must be wild with envy—it was the kind of bar he'd lusted after but hadn't been able to afford. These beauties, most of them shipped from back East more than a century ago, didn't come cheap.

Chelsea could easily imagine miners, cattlemen and gamblers bellying up to that bar in days gone by. Obviously this saloon had seen it all and then some. The band was tuning up, so the party was about to get started.

A woman wearing jeans and a Western shirt walked toward them. A long blond braid hung down her back and she moved with assurance, as if she owned the place. Chelsea was willing to bet that she did.

She confirmed it immediately. "I'm Josie Chance, and you must be Chelsea and Finn," she said as she shook hands with both of them. "Welcome to Spirits and Spurs. Thanks for escorting them over here, Pam."

"Fortunately they came peacefully." Pam grinned at them. "But if you'll excuse me, I see my darling husband over at the bar and we haven't checked in with each other in a couple of days."

Josie waved her away. "Go for it."

Chelsea noticed Pam heading toward a distinguished-looking cowboy with a gray mustache. "Has her husband been out of town?"

"No, Emmett lives at the Last Chance Ranch. He's the foreman there. They were married Christmas before last, but they maintain separate residences and get together when they can."

"That's fascinating. Don't you think so, Finn?"

"I'm sorry. What?" Apparently he hadn't heard a word because he'd been too absorbed in his surroundings.

"Never mind. Cool bar, huh?"

"It's amazing. I love this whole place, Josie. It has the kind of atmosphere I'm going for at O'Roarke's Brewhouse, but I haven't quite achieved it yet."

Josie smiled. "Give yourself another hundred years."

"That's how old it is?" Finn glanced up into the rafters. "No wonder it feels so authentic."

"And it has ghosts."

Finn's eyes narrowed. "You're kidding."

"I hope she's not." Chelsea shivered with excitement. "I've always wanted to see one."

"Well, I have seen one, right in this room after closing. I knew the saloon was supposed to be haunted by the ghosts of past patrons, so I renamed it Spirits and Spurs, thinking I was being clever. Then I saw my first ghost and realized I was being accurate."

Chelsea sucked in a breath. "That is so cool."

"That is so creepy." Finn didn't seem as happy about the ghost situation.

"Not everyone believes it." Josie shrugged. "Their choice. I know what I saw and I stand by the name. By the way, I've tasted your beer, Finn, and it's excellent. If you can guarantee me a steady supply, I'll put it on the menu."

"I'd be honored, ma'am."

"Aha! Spoken like a Wyoming boy. Nice hat, too."

"We were in coach," Chelsea said, "but the hat rode in first class. Both legs. The flight attendants were very accommodating."

"I understand how that could happen." Josie gave Finn

a speculative glance. "Women appreciate a nice hat. Anyway, I've monopolized you two long enough. The rest of the gang is sitting in the far corner where those two tables are pushed together. Let's get your drinks ordered before we go over. What'll you have?"

"O'Roarke's Pale Ale," Chelsea said, knowing it would please Finn. Besides, she liked it.

"Make that two, please." Finn said.

"Why am I not surprised?" Josie beckoned to a waitress and gave her the order before turning back to them. "Hand-crafted beers are a fun idea. I've always thought owning the saloon was good enough, but lately I've been thinking that a microbrewery would be an interesting challenge."

Finn clutched his chest. "A competitor? Right when I've snagged your business?"

"Relax." She patted him on the arm. "It'll take me ages to get up to speed. By then you'll have the entire West Coast sewed up."

"Just kidding, ma'am. I'd be glad to help any way I can. There's room for both of us."

Chelsea's heart swelled. Finn was turning into a savvy businessman, as evidenced by his decision to expand his territory. But he wasn't cutthroat about it and he was more than willing to lend a hand to a competitor. She'd admired that strength of character from the day they'd met.

Josie ushered them over to the table where the rest of the family sat, and immediately the men all pushed back their chairs and stood. Impressive. Cowboy manners were beginning to grow on her.

As Josie made the introductions, the calendar helped Chelsea identify people. She recognized Jack, Nick and Gabe instantly, and Dominique had to be the short-haired brunette sitting next to Nick. That meant Gabe's wife, Morgan, was the curvy redhead.

"Sarah and Pete will be here any minute," Josie said. "But they told us to go ahead and order food instead of waiting for them, so have a seat and grab a menu." She laughed. "I refuse to be modest. Everything's good here."

"Well, I'm starving." Chelsea sat next to Jack. That was when she noticed that everyone had a bottle of O'Roarke's Pale Ale in front of them.

Obviously, Finn had noticed it, too. He gestured toward the bottles. "That's right nice of you," he said. "I really didn't expect everyone to be obliged to drink it."

"Why not?" Nick smiled at him. "It was free!"

"Exactly. I love me a free beer." Jack raised his bottle in a subtle salute. "And it's not half-bad. If Josie goes ahead with her microbrewery plan, she'll have to step it up in order to top this. We'll have you beat on the label, though."

"I don't know about that." Finn settled into his chair with a grin. Apparently he was comfortable with this kind of teasing. "You have to admit that an Irish name on a beer bottle just looks natural."

"Maybe so, but you don't have historic information to slap on the back side." Jack turned the bottle around. "In this space here, where you can only brag about the quality of your hops and such, we get to talk about a beer inspired by the friendly spirits of Shoshone, namely, 'Ghost Drinkers in the Bar.'"

Chelsea laughed. "That's good."

"We've worked up a little ditty for the commercial." Gabe smoothed his mustache. "You oughta hear it."

Morgan rolled her eyes. "Hey, they just got here. You don't have to do this now."

"Oh, I think we do." Nick began to hum the tune for "Ghost Riders in the Sky."

Dominique glanced across the table at Chelsea and Finn. "Sorry. When they get like this it's impossible to control them."

"And why would you?" Jack stood and motioned the other two to do the same. As the band started playing the song, the three brothers began singing it, or rather a version of it.

The word *riders* became *drinkers*, who seemed to be riding bar stools instead of horses. They were also the ones with the red eyes, and instead of pounding hooves they had pounding heads. The chorus was YouTube worthy, with the guys throwing their arms around each other's shoulders and belting out the *yippee-yi-yay* part along with *ghost drinkers in the baaaaarrrr.*

Chelsea laughed so hard her sides ached. Through brimming eyes she glanced over at Finn, who was gasping for breath and wiping his eyes. She hadn't seen him have so much fun in…forever.

When the men sat down again, Finn cleared his throat. "I give. With that kind of promo, Spirits and Spurs beer is going to dominate the market."

Jack smiled at him. "I know."

"Don't count yourself out yet, Finn," Chelsea said. "Don't forget your ace in the hole."

He glanced over at her. "What's that?"

"Me."

3

"GOOD POINT." Finn had loved watching Chelsea crack up. Her cheeks glowed pink and her lashes were spiked with tears of laughter. "Gentlemen, I take back what I said. With Chelsea in my corner, I can face any comers."

Jack nodded. "I could tell from the moment I laid eyes on her that she would be a worthy opponent. Never underestimate a woman with purple streaks in her hair."

"Lavender," Chelsea shot back.

"See what I mean?" Jack waved a hand in her direction. "She'll stand up to anyone, even me. So, are we all gonna eat or dance?"

"Both!" called out a male voice.

Finn turned in his chair as a tall, fit man who was probably in his seventies walked toward them with a silver-haired woman who had the bearing of a queen. Finn stood, as did all the men at the table. Sarah Chance was in the building, along with her husband of only a few years, Pete Beckett.

They came over immediately to the newcomers, and Chelsea rose from her chair to greet them. "I can't tell you how excited I am about tomorrow," Chelsea said. "Thank you for hosting this event."

"Yes, thank you, ma'am." Finn looked into blue eyes that shone with intelligence and wisdom. He'd heard that Sarah was a special woman, and after only a minute or so of being in her presence, he understood why people said that. She gave off enough warmth and good humor to envelop everyone at the table, but Finn suspected she was also capable of silencing the entire group with a look.

Pete glanced around the table. "Have you ordered?"

"Not yet." Morgan tossed back her red hair and gave her husband a pointed look. "Some people had to subject us all, including our guests, to 'Ghost Drinkers.'"

"I see." Pete rubbed a hand over his face as if hiding a smile. "Chelsea and Finn, I'd like to say that was an aberration, but I'm afraid things like that go on all the time around here."

"I hope so," Chelsea said.

"But not while you give your presentation." Jack patted her shoulder. "You have my word that we'll behave ourselves tomorrow afternoon."

"But once everyone leaves, all bets are off." Nick winked at her. "I have a feeling you can take it."

"Oh, she can." Finn felt compelled to alert them. "She can also dish it out, so watch yourselves."

"I figured as much," Jack said. "But didn't you say you were starving, Chelsea? We'd better rustle up some grub. Then we can dance while we wait for it." He glanced over at Finn. "I assume you dance?"

"Depends on your definition."

"Hmm." Jack didn't look impressed by the response. "I hope you're not into salsa."

"Only with my chips."

"That's a relief." Jack returned his attention to his menu. "Don't know why I bother looking at this. I know it by heart. Give me your order, everybody. I'll relay it to the cook."

"I can call Heather over," Josie said. "You don't have to play waiter."

"Heather's running herself ragged tonight. I know the menu, probably better than she does. I can do it."

Finn decided that he liked Jack. The guy had a sense of humor, but he also wasn't afraid to pitch in when necessary. Finn had done the same many times at O'Roarke's Brewhouse. Josie was the owner here, but Jack obviously tried to lighten her load.

After he disappeared with their order, Sarah cast a glance at her remaining sons and daughters-in-law. "I checked on the kids before we left and Cassidy seems to have everything under control."

"Good," Josie said.

"Thank God for Cassidy." Morgan looked over at Chelsea and Finn. "My youngest sister. She's the ranch housekeeper and she babysits the grandkids, although now that she has a boyfriend we have to make sure we plan ahead."

Jack returned and pulled his wife out of her chair. "I have a plan. I finally have a night out with the woman of my dreams. Let's hit the floor, lady."

"I like that idea a lot." Gabe offered his hand to Morgan. "Dance with me?"

"As long as you don't sing in my ear." But Morgan looked happy as she joined her husband on the floor.

Nick and Dominique followed, and Pete stood and held Sarah's chair. He paused when Finn and Chelsea didn't immediately leave the table. "How about you two?"

"We'll be out there in a minute," Finn said.

"You're sure?" Sarah hesitated. "We don't want to leave our guests sitting all alone."

"We're right behind you." Finn grabbed his beer bottle and glanced at Chelsea. "I don't know about you, but I need some Dutch courage."

"I'm with you." She took several swallows. "Okay, let's do this thing."

Finn didn't feel ready, but Chelsea was on her feet. He pushed back his chair. "I don't know a lot about dancing, but that looks like what they call country swing. It's fairly popular around here."

"Whatever you say. I'm pretty much clueless." Chelsea studied the participants. "Lots of twirling and fancy footwork. But we might be able to fake it."

"My specialty is standing in one spot and shuffling around."

"That's not going to work, Finn. They'll run you over."

"Should we reconsider? After all, you do have on sandals. If I don't squash your toes I'm liable to place you in serious danger from somebody else. We could sit and drink beer, instead."

"No, we need to try it. Maybe if we spin around a lot nobody will notice we don't know what we're doing."

Finn sucked in a breath. "All right. Let's go." At the edge of the dance floor he grabbed Chelsea and began madly twirling her around the perimeter. He stepped on her a couple of times, but she didn't yell, so it must not have hurt too much.

On his second circuit, Jack showed up beside them and grabbed his shoulder hard enough to stop the twirling. "What the hell is that you're doing?"

Finn decided to brave it out. "The same thing you're doing."

"I think not." He gently set Chelsea aside. "Stay right here, sweetheart. I'll bring him back in a few minutes."

"Hang on." Finn stepped back, both hands raised. "Whatever you have in mind, I'm not doing it."

"Work with me, O'Roarke." Jack grasped his hand.

Finn pulled free. "I'm not dancing with you, Jack."

"You weren't dancing with Chelsea, either. You have two choices. You can continue to look like an idiot out on the floor or you can let me give you a quick lesson."

"Three choices. I can head back to the table and drink."

"You're a quitter? Is that what you're saying? I didn't peg you for a quitter."

Those were the magic words. Finn sighed. "Tell me what to do."

"That's better. Put your hand around my waist. Pretend I'm Chelsea."

"She doesn't have a five o'clock shadow."

"And she has way fancier hair and I'm sure she smells better, too. Just focus on what I'm telling you. The idea is to describe a box with your feet and turn at the same time. Now go."

"You do realize this will look ridiculous."

"It's no worse than the hot mess you were a bit ago. Come on, now, you built your own business. That takes cojones. This is just a little dancing."

Finn could have used more beer, but if Jack was willing to make a fool of himself, then, what the hell? Might as well go along. Good thing nobody he knew was here except Chelsea. Having her watch was bad enough, but at least she'd admitted that she wasn't very good, either.

Then he caught movement on the far side of the dance floor and realized Josie was dancing with Chelsea. "Hey! Your wife is dancing with my..." He trailed off, unable to come up with a proper title for her.

"Your what?" Jack exerted pressure on Finn's shoulder to keep him moving in the right direction. "I'm no expert, but I feel a vibe between you two."

"She's my business associate."

"Yeah, and I'm Elvis. Tell me another one. And lead with your other foot. There. That's better. Good."

"I can't believe I'm doing this."

"Anybody who owns a hat like yours should be able to dance the two-step. I think you have the basics. Josie's coming around again with your *business associate*. We'll trade partners."

And just like that, Jack thrust him into Chelsea's arms and the momentum kept them moving around the floor. Miraculously, they were even doing it in a synchronized fashion. "I'm not sure what just happened."

"I think it was the fastest dancing lesson in history."

"Embarrassing as it is to admit, Jack's a good teacher."

"Josie said he's considered the dancing master at the Last Chance. He's working with the kids now so that they'll grow up knowing how."

"You were right that it's an important skill around here. And believe it or not, we might be actually doing it. More or less. Sort of."

"We might." She smiled as she gazed up at him. "I can't remember the last time I've had so much fun."

"You know what? Me, either." He wanted to tell her that she was the most beautiful woman in the world, but instead he twirled her around one more time and the music ended.

Jack came by and leaned toward them. "Good job. Now let's eat."

The food, as Josie had mentioned, was excellent. Finn noted that the pub fries were better than what he served at O'Roarke's. Humbling, because he was proud of his establishment's pub fries, but this little saloon in Wyoming did them better.

After dinner everyone danced some more. Jack suggested that he partner Chelsea while Josie partnered Finn. Finn improved a lot while dancing with Josie, but he was grateful once Chelsea was back in his arms.

He was comforted knowing that she wasn't any more accomplished than he was, but that wasn't the only reason he liked dancing with her. He'd discovered how much he loved holding her.

She felt so right cradled in his arms. He should have guessed that she would. The warmth in her eyes told him she felt the same way. This trip was designed to deliver a Hail Mary pass that would clinch the Kickstarter project and save the ranch. No small potatoes, there. But already it felt as if even more was at stake.

As the evening progressed, Jack kept bringing over more O'Roarke's Pale Ale. Finn knew his inhibitions were disappearing, and he could tell from the way Chelsea danced with him that hers were, too. He had to stay strong.

She'd made it obvious months ago that she thought they could have a lot of fun together. He completely agreed with her. But starting an affair with her had the potential to make him forget everything else. They had an important mission to accomplish this weekend, and he couldn't let anything distract him from that.

Dancing with her was safe enough, though. They had people all around them and he still had to concentrate on his footwork so he wouldn't step on her or run into other couples. That left him very little time to think about how soft her breasts felt or how perfectly their hips aligned thanks to her high-heeled sandals.

Then they goaded each other into attempting a very

fast number. They made a mess of it, but he was proud of them for trying. When the music ended they clung to each other, laughing and gasping for breath.

Gradually he realized he could feel the rapid thump of her heart as she leaned against his chest. His palm, which was flattened against the small of her back, rotated in a slow massage. He hadn't been conscious of doing it at first. He looked down at her and she was looking right back at him, her full lips parted as she sucked in air.

The heat of her body was nothing compared to the heat in her gaze. On cue, his groin tightened. He released her slowly and stepped back as he fought to control his reaction. He hoped she hadn't noticed, but when the corners of her mouth tilted up a fraction, he thought she had. Maybe dancing with her wasn't so safe, after all.

Just his luck, the party broke up after that. Pam came over to tell them she was going back to the Last Chance so she could spend the night with her husband. Breakfast would be served as usual because her housekeeper, Yvonne, was also the cook.

Several people offered Chelsea and Finn a ride back to the Bunk and Grub, but Finn suggested walking and Chelsea quickly agreed. He couldn't speak for her, but he needed a cooling-off period before stepping into a cozy B and B where his room was right next to hers.

At least he hadn't brought condoms. He was grateful for that as they walked through the cool night air. Fortunately the thought hadn't crossed his mind in connection with this trip, and even if it had, he would have made sure *not* to have any.

"That was fun." Chelsea's heels clicked on the sidewalk, a sharper sound than what his boots made. "I expected to like them and I do."

"Me, too. Great family. I have a good feeling about tomorrow. Their support could put us over the top."

"Yep." She wrapped her arms around herself. "It's kind of nippy out here."

"Yeah." This cooling-off period had turned out to be just plain cold. If he'd had a coat, he would have given it to her, but he didn't, and taking off his shirt would be ridiculous. He felt the chill, too, after all that dancing in a warm room. Her blouse was flimsy compared to his cotton shirt, so she must be freezing.

From the corner of his eye he could see her struggling not to shiver. Aw, hell, he had to do something about that. "Don't take this the wrong way, but I'm going to put my arm around you so you won't be cold."

"That would b-be lovely."

"I didn't think about how the temperature drops at night in late August." He kept his tone nonchalant as he wrapped his arm around her shoulders and matched his stride to hers. "Warm during the day and frosty at night."

"S-so I see." Nestling against him, she slid her arm around his waist. "Thanks."

And he was no longer cold. She fit against his side and synchronized her steps to his as if they'd walked this way hundreds of times. He tightened his grip on her warm, firm shoulder and imagined touching her warm, firm skin.

Oh, God, now he was thinking of what else they could do that would be effortless. Kissing, for example. And then sliding out of their clothes and into a bed, either his or hers. The more turned on he became the faster he walked. He didn't realize it until he heard their labored breathing.

He slowed down. "Sorry. Didn't mean to start race-walking."

"That's okay." There was a hint of laughter in her voice. "Good way to warm up."

He could think of another good way. In fact, that seemed to be the only thing he could think about.

She stopped making conversation and so did he. No telling what would come out of his mouth in his current state.

Her scent teased him with possibilities. Her hair swung as they walked, brushing his shoulder. He wanted to thread his fingers through those silky strands, cup the back of her head and finally taste the lips he'd stared at for years. *Years, damn it!*

Instead of kissing her, he let her go when they reached the B and B's porch steps so he could dig out his keys. As it turned out, she got to hers first and opened the front door.

He followed her into the silent entry. A trace of cinnamon hung in the warm air and a Tiffany-style lamp glowed in the parlor. Etched-crystal sconces along the stairway created an intriguing mix of light and shadow. He remembered they were alone on the second floor of the house. No other guests.

Chelsea started up the carpeted steps and he followed, keeping a safe distance behind her. No, there wasn't such a thing as a safe distance. He watched hungrily as her snug jeans lovingly stretched over her backside as she climbed. Even though he'd slowed his pace, his heart thumped as if they'd run the whole way.

Rational thought drifted away as insanity gripped him. Her hand on the polished railing made him think of her hand on his cock. The lack of condoms was no longer a lucky circumstance that would keep him from doing something stupid. It was a damned inconvenience standing between him and paradise.

Neither of his best friends would have been caught in this situation. Yet here he was, aching for someone who would probably welcome him into her bed if he gave the slightest indication that he wanted to be there, and he was condomless.

Pausing at her door, she inserted the key in the lock. His fevered brain attached a sexual connotation to that, too.

But there would be no inserting anything because he was without those little raincoats.

She glanced at him as he approached her. Her face was in shadow, her expression hidden. "See you in the morning." Twisting the key, she opened her door and started through it. Lamplight from inside the room skimmed her tempting silhouette.

He was pushed beyond reason into a world of primitive needs. Even as unprepared as he was, he couldn't let her go. "Wait."

She turned and peered up at him. "Finn, are you okay?"

"No." His voice rasped in the stillness.

"What's the matter?"

"I…" He stopped to clear the huskiness from his throat. "I want you so much I can't breathe."

"Oh." Her beautiful mouth curved in a smile and she stepped back from the door. "Would you like to come in?"

"God, yes, but I…I didn't anticipate this."

"I'm sure you didn't."

Hope dawned. "Did you?"

"No, of course not."

He groaned. "Then we can't—"

"Maybe not *that*, but there are alternatives."

Alternatives. The word stood out in flashing neon in his frazzled brain.

Curling her fingers into the front of his shirt, she pulled him slowly inside her room. "You haven't dated since Alison. I haven't dated since I asked you out. Do you understand what I'm saying?"

Swallowing, he nodded.

"Good." She took off his hat and laid it on the dresser. "Because I can hardly wait to get my hands on you, Finn O'Roarke."

He had the presence of mind to kick the door shut before his brain shut down completely.

4

CHELSEA HAD TRIED to be good. She really had tried, except for her earlier remark about the foot rub. When they'd had their hot moment on the dance floor, she hadn't teased him about the hard ridge she'd felt pressed against her belly before he'd backed away.

He wanted to keep his distance, and she had vowed to honor that. She would have suffered the cold air on the walk home in silence because it was her own fault for not bringing a jacket. But then he'd wrapped his arm around her. The moment she'd felt his touch and the delicious heat of his body, a fantasy movie had started rolling in her head.

And now—against all odds—fantasy had become reality. Flattening her palms against his chest, she absorbed the wild beating of his heart as he combed his fingers through her hair and tilted her head back. His gaze moved hungrily over her face and settled on her mouth. He groaned. "Chelsea…" And then he was there, his velvet lips covering hers.

At last. Joy surged through her at the urgent pressure of his mouth and the deliberate thrust of his tongue. Oh, yes, this was good, and right, and ahhh…he could kiss better than any man she'd ever known.

He angled his head and went deeper, inspiring shocking thoughts about where else she wanted that talented mouth. He obviously knew what she'd meant when she'd suggested alternatives. They had all night, but that didn't mean they shouldn't get started on that program ASAP.

She wrenched apart the snaps of his shirt, desperate to touch him. When she laid both hands against his muscled chest and stroked him there, he shuddered and lifted his mouth from hers. "I'm going crazy." He gulped for air. "I have zero control."

"That's okay." Pulse hammering, she slid her hand down to his zipper. Oh, my. What she'd felt on the dance floor had been a mere prelude. "I'll just—"

"No, it's not okay." He caught her hand and brought it up to his mouth. His breathing ragged, he kissed her fingertips one by one. "We're changing focus."

"To what?"

His blue eyes glowed with intensity. "You."

She gasped as a fresh wave of lust crashed over her. Her attention shifted to his mouth and her imagination kicked into high gear. She began to tremble. "I could live with that."

His soft laughter gave her goose bumps. "Ah, Chels. You're one of a kind."

"And don't you forget it."

He held her gaze. "I never have." Then he stepped back and looked her up and down, as if evaluating his next move. His attention settled on the belt circling her hips. "How does that come off?"

"Easy." But eagerness made her clumsy and she messed it up somehow. She swore softly and kept working at the clasp.

"Let me see." He knelt in front of her, moved her hands aside and had the belt undone in two seconds. As it slithered to the floor he slipped both hands under the hem of her tunic and before she could take a breath he'd unbuttoned her jeans.

As he started pulling them down, panties and all, her heart beat so fast she grew dizzy. "My…my shoes."

"You get the blouse." His voice rasped in the stillness. "I'll get the shoes." He unbuckled the straps and slipped off one shoe at a time, taking care that she didn't lose her balance. His touch was nimble, practiced and incredibly erotic.

"You're…" She paused to gulp in air. "You're good at that."

"Cowboy stuff."

At first she didn't get it and then she understood. Bridles, halters, harnesses—leather and buckles were no challenge to a man with cowboy skills.

He tenderly divested her of her jeans and panties, too. Still on his knees, he caressed her calves and gradually made his way up her quaking thighs. His questing fingers drew closer to the spot where she ached so fiercely that she barely contained a whimper of longing. She closed her eyes to savor his touch.

Then he paused.

She moaned softly. "Don't stop."

"Your blouse."

"Oh." He'd mesmerized her so completely that she'd forgotten her assignment. Grabbing the hem, she whipped the shirt over her head, then took off her bra and flung it after the blouse. Her breasts ached for his touch, too.

With a sharp intake of breath, he rose and stepped back.

She watched him and was thrilled by his awestruck

reaction. Lifting her chin, she looked him in the eye. "See what you've been missing?"

His gaze roved over her. "Yes." His chest heaved. "And I'm a damned fool."

"Not tonight."

"No, not tonight. Thank God for alternatives." And with a swiftness that made her squeal, he swept her up in his arms and laid her on the bed. Then he pulled off his clothes with utter disregard for where they landed. That was so unlike Finn.

Her tidy little Victorian room took on the appearance of a ravishing. She was more than ready to be ravished, even if his options for accomplishing that were limited. But when she had her first unobstructed view of his package, she cursed the lack of condoms.

She'd thought fleetingly about bringing them, but that had seemed like tempting fate. If she'd brought them and then had taken the box home unopened, she would have needed more than a few bottles of O'Roarke's Pale Ale to get over her disappointment.

But, oh, how she yearned for what he had to offer. "O'Roarke, I have one thing to say."

"Only one?"

"Yes." Viewing that kind of male beauty and knowing there were restrictions on enjoying it made her impatient. "Before tomorrow night, we'll obtain a box of condoms."

"It's a small town, don't forget. Word spreads."

"I don't care."

He grinned. "You know what? Neither do I."

If there was ever a more stirring sight than Finn naked and smiling, she'd never seen it. Her fantasies of him paled in comparison to the real man, his erect cock seated in a cloud of dark hair and his impressive balls tight with desire. Better yet, she'd inspired this aroused condition.

No matter what happened after tonight, she'd carry that potent image with her.

He walked over to the bed. "Make room. I'm coming in."

"I sort of expected that." She scooted over and patted the spot next to her. "Here you go."

"Thanks." He climbed onto the bed and immediately moved over her, rolling her to her back in the process. "For the next little while, we'll be pretty much occupying the same area."

Somewhere along the way he'd changed his attitude. Outside her door he'd been desperate yet hesitant to fully commit. Now he was all in. This new, more masterful Finn thrilled her to her toes. "You say that as if you're in charge."

"Not necessarily." He leaned down and nibbled at her mouth. "But I think you'd like it if I took over."

Oh, yes, she certainly would. "How did you know?"

"Lucky guess."

And as he captured her mouth and cupped her breast in a slow, sensuous massage, she abandoned herself to the sensation of letting Finn be in charge. What a heady feeling, turning her body over to a man. She couldn't recall ever doing that. In vulnerable situations, she preferred to be in control.

But it was no mystery why she could surrender so completely to him. His sense of honesty and fair play was bone deep. She'd known that from the moment they'd met. She trusted him more than any man she'd ever been naked with.

And because of that trust, she allowed herself to let go in a way that she never would have with someone else. As he ran his hands over her curves, she arched into his caress with a moan of delight. When he cradled her breasts so that he could use his mouth to drive her crazy, she let herself make all the noise she wanted to.

The pleasure he gave her was more intense because it was Finn. Finn was the man kissing his way down the valley between her breasts and over her quivering stomach. Finn was the man parting her thighs, the man who was about to bestow the most intimate of kisses.

His knowing touch made her gasp as he explored and stroked with clever fingers. His breath was warm against her damp skin and she trembled in silent anticipation. With the first swipe of his tongue, she cried out, electrified by the moist pressure on the most sensitive spot of all.

He did it again, drawing out the motion, and she sucked in a breath. "More."

He obviously knew the meaning of *more*. In seconds she was writhing on the bed thanks to the wonder of Finn's mouth. His hands bracketing her hips, he lifted her up so he could sink deeper, take more. He was definitely ravishing her. And she loved it.

She came in a rush, her breathless cries filling the small room. If she'd expected him to stop there, she'd underestimated him. He teased and taunted her until she spiraled out of control a second time. She forgot where she was as she spun in a whirlpool of sensation.

But she never forgot who was loving her. Finn O'Roarke was in bed with her at last, and the results were more spectacular than she could have imagined. But as he left her quaking center and returned to place a lingering kiss on her mouth, she reminded herself that alternatives included fun for both parties.

Disengaging was no easy task because he seemed to really like kissing her and she really liked him kissing her. But she had other plans for her mouth. Cupping his face in both hands, she pushed upward until he lifted his head. "My turn," she murmured, looking into his passion-glazed eyes. They'd never seemed quite so blue.

"But I love making you come. I'm just taking a short break. You taste so good. I want to—"

"No. *My turn.* I mean it."

He smiled. "I can tell. Your eyes are shooting sparks."

"Fair is fair." She ran her tongue slowly over her lips. "And I think you'll have fun."

As he stared at her mouth, his breathing changed.

"Think about how nice it will feel when I use my tongue on your—"

He groaned. "Lord help me, I want that."

"Of course you do. We're shifting the focus to you, O'Roarke."

Dragging in a breath, he stretched out beside her. "This won't take long."

"Are you sure?" She straddled his thighs, feeling more uninhibited than ever in her life. She embraced showmanship in her job, but she'd never felt motivated to practice it in the bedroom. Two orgasms and a naked Finn stretched beneath her had turned her into a seductress.

"Absolutely sure." His chest rose and fell rapidly and he clenched his jaw. "I've wanted you for five years."

"Ditto." His rigid cock was directly in front of her, magnificently erect with a drop of moisture gathered at the tip. She grasped the base of his penis and squeezed gently. "And now I have you, at least for tonight. If you prop some pillows behind your head you can watch me making you happy."

He gasped. "Dangerous. I already feel as if I could come any second."

"You won't if I keep pressure here." She tightened the

circle created by her fingers and the muscles in his jaw gradually relaxed.

"That…helps."

"Good. I want you to be able to savor this. Grab those pillows, Finn."

He reached for a couple and stuffed them behind his head.

She smiled. "Excellent." Leaning down, she kept her fingers in place as she licked the tiny bead of moisture away.

He moaned. "Chelsea. That's…"

Another drop appeared and she licked that, too.

He swore softly.

She glanced up. "Good visual?"

"You have no idea." His voice was strained.

"Just keep watching." She retained her firm grip as she closed her mouth over his cock.

He gasped and fisted his hands in the coverlet. "Go easy."

She'd planned on that. He might not think he could last, but she wanted to draw out the pleasure as long as possible. Predictably, though, the earthy, salty taste of him tightened the coil of desire deep in her belly. Apparently two orgasms weren't enough for her, at least not when she was with Finn.

But she'd declared that this was his turn, so she ignored her own needs and concentrated on his. That wasn't a simple task. As she inched down the hot, tight length of him, her inner muscles clenched in protest. *Tomorrow night*, she vowed.

Tonight she'd love him this way—flattening her tongue to put more pressure along the sensitive vein and hollowing her cheeks as she drew him in. At last the tip of his cock touched the back of her throat.

She moved slowly up and down, and with each swirl of her tongue his breathing grew more labored. He swore again, his words a little more graphic. Despite the restriction she'd created with her fingers, he wouldn't be able to hold back much longer.

Sliding up to the tip, she treated him to some lollipop licks that produced a tortured groan. She followed with easy, deliberate suction. Gradually she became more energetic and he began to pant.

"Chelsea...please..."

She recognized that tone of desperation. Releasing the tight coil created by her fingers, she plunged downward and sucked hard.

He erupted with a deep-throated groan of release. She gloried in that sound, so full of joy and satisfaction. She'd longed to see him break his self-imposed chains, and for this moment, he had.

She swallowed every drop, and when he finally relaxed against the bed, she shimmied up his chest and gave him an open-mouthed kiss. With a soft moan, he embraced her and returned that kiss with an energy that surprised her. She would have expected him to be worn out.

Instead he was using his tongue in ways that reminded her of her own needs and the urges she'd put aside while she made love to him. If she didn't know better, she'd think he was tempting her on purpose. When he thrust his tongue deep into her mouth, she whimpered.

With gentle pressure, he lifted her mouth a fraction away from his. "Slide on up here where I can reach you." His seductive request was delivered in a low, husky voice.

She shivered. Since he could already reach her mouth just fine, that left only one other possibility. Heat sluiced through her as she considered that bold move.

They'd progressed from their first kiss ever to X-rated

positions in a very short time. But unexpressed lust had been simmering between them for five years, so maybe their erotic behavior tonight wasn't a surprise, after all.

"Come on, Chels." His voice was like velvet stroking her nerve endings. "Let me taste you again."

"You could make me come just talking that way."

"I'd rather make you come with my mouth and my tongue. You want that, too. I can feel you trembling."

"I do want that." Decision made, she pushed herself up until she was sitting on his chest. Then she leaned over and grasped the brass headboard.

His big hands supporting her hips, he coaxed her into position and…she lost her mind. Lying on the bed in a state of surrender had been incredible, but now she was a more active participant. Holding on to the headboard for support, she could rock forward or back. She could silently ask for anything she wanted from him.

It was like a dance, only she was leading and he was following her every cue. She imagined him as her love slave dedicated to giving her pleasure. And he did…oh, how he did. She moaned, she gasped and at last she cried out as her climax roared through her.

As the quaking finally slowed, he guided her down beside him again. Then he gathered her close and they lay tangled together, unable to move. Eventually a chill in the room convinced them to climb under the covers.

Chelsea had never felt so satisfied and relaxed in her life. With her fingers laced through his, she drifted in a haze of sensual delight. Before she fell asleep, she had one last thought. If loving Finn was like this, she wanted more of it.

5

FINN WOKE UP the next morning with a smile on his face and a song in his heart. That lasted about two seconds and then it occurred to him that he was a complete a-hole. Making sweet love to Chelsea had been the best experience of his life, but it hadn't changed the way he thought about their situation.

If anything, their incredible sexual experience had underscored the problem. His foster parents had a serious situation that deserved all his attention. He certainly hadn't been thinking about it last night.

But even if he rededicated himself to that issue, he'd introduced sex into his relationship with Chelsea, and there was no going back. Now they both knew how great it could be, but he couldn't imagine having an affair, especially with a high-voltage woman like her, and still run his business effectively. So what was he doing in her bed now, when he had his foster parents to think of and no intention of following through with Chelsea once they returned to Seattle?

"That's some frown you're wearing for so early in the morning."

He turned onto his side and discovered she was watching him. "I just figured out what a total jerk I am." And to make matters worse, seeing her lying there facing him with her brown gaze soft and one creamy breast barely covered by the sheet, he wanted to do it all over again. Twice.

Then she smiled, which added one more element of delicious appeal. "I've shared that opinion of you a few times in the past, but right now I'm feeling quite complimentary. You're a wonderful lover, in case no one's ever mentioned that before. You're intuitive, and generous and—"

"And not fit to wipe your boots, let alone climb in to your bed." He'd love to blame the alcohol, but the cold walk home had sobered him up. He'd known exactly what he was doing.

"My goodness!" She propped her head on her hand. "What brought on the self-loathing? You seemed rather pleased with yourself when we went to sleep. As well you should be after—"

"That wasn't right."

"Oh, yes it was. You were absolutely on target every time. You left me wrung out with pleasure." Her brown eyes narrowed. "I can't believe you're the kind of guy who turns prudish in the light of day."

"Nope." If only she knew that under the sheet he was ramrod stiff. "It's taking all my willpower not to reach for you right this minute. But instead I need to apologize for last night."

"What, you should have given me *more* orgasms? You have higher standards than I thought."

"My standards suck. I should never have set foot in this room. I wanted you so much that I made a selfish decision. Because I did, you could logically think I've changed my mind about us, but I haven't."

She met that declaration with silence as if processing what he'd said. Then she took a deep breath. "That doesn't surprise me."

"It doesn't?" He'd expected anger, not this calm acceptance.

"No, not really. I wouldn't have minded waking up to find that you'd seen the light and that you think we should find out where this relationship takes us. I was willing to believe it might happen. Some guys are swayed by damned good sex."

"It was damned good sex. The best ever. But—"

"You still have a business to run." She said it with exactly the same inflection he would have used.

If she wanted to mock him, that was no more than he deserved. "Yeah." He felt like a piece of gum on the bottom of her shoe. "But that's not even all of it. I should be thinking about my foster parents' situation, not giving in to my lust. I'm sorry, Chels. I'll get the hell out of your bed as soon as this erection goes down a little and I can get dressed without maiming myself."

To his amazement she smiled, and the smile turned into a chuckle that became a belly laugh. She flopped to her back and giggled uncontrollably.

"What's so funny?" He'd anticipated she might start throwing things and instead she was laughing hysterically.

"You are!"

"Oh, that's nice. Laugh at the guy with a boner. Actually, though, you're doing me a favor. Yep, I'm much better already. Nothing like having a woman laugh at your willy to make it return to normal." He threw back the covers and got out of bed.

"Wait." She gulped back another giggle and hopped out on the other side. "I wasn't laughing about that. Well, in a way I was, but it was more because you're so adorable."

He barely heard that last part. He was too busy staring at her as the light of early morning caressed her pale skin, giving her a faint glow. Her rosy nipples tightened under his gaze. They seemed to tilt slightly upward, as if inviting him to taste them again.

He longed to span her narrow waist with both hands, to kneel before her and pay homage to that downy blond triangle where he'd spent so much quality time last night. He'd love to revisit that special place now that the sun was rising.

That wasn't the only thing rising, either.

She glanced at his cock and then looked into his eyes. "Finn, I know you think it's unfair to get sexually involved with me on this trip that's supposed to be about your foster parents, especially when you plan to drop me like a hot potato when we get home."

"That's because it *is* unfair. I'm not that kind of guy."

"I know you're not. You're driven and ambitious, but you're not a user."

"That's not true, either. I used Alison and I'll never forgive myself for that."

"Used her? Near as I could tell, she honed in on you like a heat-seeking missile."

"I admit she was determined, but that doesn't excuse my decision to accept her proposal."

"She proposed? I didn't know that, but I'm not too surprised."

"She did, but I could have turned her down." He hated saying it out loud, but she needed to know all the ugly truths about him. "Instead I agreed to marry her because I thought she was a safe alternative to you."

"What?"

"You're the most exciting woman I've ever met. If we started dating, I'd abandon my business so I could spend more time with you."

"You would not! I—"

"Look at how I reacted last night!" He swept a hand toward his stiff cock. "How I'm reacting right now. You turn me on like no one else. I could so easily become obsessed with you. I knew I'd never become obsessed with Alison and I thought..." He rubbed the back of his neck. "This is really hard to say."

"Then don't."

"No, I need to. If you understand how rotten I am, you'll stay away. I knew that something had to change, so I thought if I had a normal, domesticated life with Alison, I'd get over wanting you. It didn't work. She's a nice person, but—"

"She's *not* nice. She walked off with that huge settlement, which was way too much considering she did nothing to build the business. And she took your dog and your cat."

"She deserves the settlement, the two animals and a lot more. I think she knew in her heart that I used her as a substitute for you, and she was furious. She had every right to be."

Chelsea swallowed. "I knew you were attracted to me, but I had no idea how much."

"Or what lengths I would go to in order to create a barrier between us."

"Finn, I'm not that scary. Honest." She started toward him.

"No, you're wonderful. I'm the one with the issues." He should turn away and get dressed, but he was mesmerized by her lithe body as she slowly approached. "I can't take a chance that I'll ignore my foster parents and their problems. Or somehow lose O'Roarke's because I'm distracted."

"You won't do that." She moved closer. "I know how much you care about Rosie and Herb and I've seen the dedication you bring to your business. You won't allow yourself to be distracted."

"If you're right, then I'd end up shortchanging you. You should have a guy who can give you all the attention you deserve."

"You certainly did last night." She stopped when the blatant evidence of his arousal nudged her belly. "And we have a little time before breakfast."

He groaned. "We have to stop this."

"Look, at the moment there's nothing you can do about either the ranch or your business, so why not give yourself permission to have fun?"

"Because it's not fair to you."

"Let me be the judge of that." She wrapped her fingers around his all-too-willing cock. "Come back to bed with me. Let's play."

He caved. What guy wouldn't? But as he once again explored the wonders of her body, a little voice whispered that this was a prime example. With Chelsea, it was all or nothing. She was his Kryptonite and he indulged himself at his peril.

They ended up missing breakfast entirely. But when Finn opened her door intending to go to his room to shower and shave, he found a tray with a carafe of hot coffee, two mugs and a basket of pastries. He brought the tray back into the room and they sat on the bed to eat.

Chelsea picked up a croissant. "I could get used to the bed-and-breakfast lifestyle."

"This particular bed-and-breakfast, especially. The cinnamon rolls remind me of my grandfather." The moment he'd said it, he wished he hadn't. He blamed the cozy atmosphere they'd created with sex and breakfast in bed for that unintentional revelation.

She knew about his life at Thunder Mountain Ranch and that he'd landed there when his grandfather had died, leaving him without any living relatives. But he'd never talked about the man who'd raised him from the time Finn was three until he'd died of a heart attack when Finn was thirteen. The memories were so bittersweet—more bitter than sweet, really.

"He liked cinnamon rolls?"

"Loved them. It was our Sunday-morning treat from the bakery down the street."

"Nice memory." She smiled at him.

No it wasn't, because his grandfather had never had quite enough cash to pay for the cinnamon rolls. He'd played on the sympathy of the counter clerk to discount the purchase because of the hungry boy standing beside him. Finn had loved the pastries but he'd hated the serving of pity that had come with them.

Only four people in the world knew about that humiliation as well as the many others that had been part of living with a man who had been terrible with money. Cade Gallagher and Damon Harrison—the other two members of the exclusive group they called the Thunder Mountain Brotherhood—knew. And so did Rosie and Herb.

"You got really quiet all of a sudden." Chelsea gazed at him with an expression that said she wouldn't pry, but she was ready to listen if he wanted to talk.

In the end, it seemed silly not to tell her about his grandpa. After all, he and Chelsea had been business partners for five years, and in the past few hours they'd... oh, yes, they certainly had. They'd torn down some bar-

ricades, and he wondered if he'd ever be able to recon-
struct them.

"My Grandpa O'Roarke was a failure." He gauged her
reaction and could see she was gearing up to refute that.
"Yes, he gave me shelter when there was no one else, and
I'm grateful. But he barely managed to keep us housed
and fed because he was so busy chasing every get-rich
scheme he encountered."

Understanding was reflected in her eyes. "That ex-
plains a lot."

"I'm sure it does. His favorite dream was to own his
own pub. That's probably not unusual for an Irishman,
and I so desperately wanted him to succeed. But he didn't
have it in him, and I was just a kid. I couldn't see where
he was going wrong."

"I'll bet you do now."

"Yep. He won a little money in a lottery. If he'd invested it well, he might have been able to open that pub.
But he'd invested it poorly and given the rest to a friend
who was about to be evicted."

She sipped her coffee. "So he was generous, like you."

"Generosity is great if you can pay your own rent. If
you can't, then you end up asking the landlord to give
you a break. You end up talking the baker into letting you
have cinnamon rolls for half price because your grand-
son loves them so."

She regarded him silently for a moment. "And you
hated that."

"I did."

"I'm so glad you told me about this. I didn't know
what was behind your plan to open O'Roarke's Brewhouse. Now I do."

"Maybe I should have told you sooner."

She shook her head. "We had to get to this point first."

"Meaning that we had to get naked?"

"In a way. But more than being naked, which has been an excellent experience, by the way, I needed to see your disciplined approach to your business. What if you'd confessed all this that first day in the coffee shop?"

He thought about it. "I would have sounded like a nutcase, as if my entire goal was to create a business my grandfather would have loved and make it work the way he couldn't."

She didn't say a word, simply looked at him.

"And that is my goal, pretty much." The realization hummed through his veins. "I've never fully admitted that and certainly haven't said it to anyone else, but that's it. I want to do what he couldn't, both for him and for me."

"And you have."

"Thanks to you." He'd never been more aware of his debt to her than he was now.

"I wouldn't jeopardize what you've accomplished."

"Not knowingly." Even though he should be sexually satisfied, he had only to glance over at her sitting across from him on the bed and his thoughts turned to warm skin and hot kisses. They had an important assignment this weekend, and yet being with her had become a priority.

Her expression was soft with compassion. "Believe it or not, I can be the voice of reason."

"I sure do hope so, because I'm quickly discovering that when sex with you is an option, I'm the voice of what-the-hell."

"You're not used to letting go. To use a horse analogy, you've been keeping yourself penned up. It's logical that when you jump the fence for the first time, you'll go a little crazy."

"Oh, you think so?" He took her mug, put it on the tray

and moved everything to the bedside table. "I'll show you how crazy I am, lady." And he tackled her, making her giggle as he pushed her down on the soft sheets.

Then he held her arms above her head while he placed butterfly kisses on her cheeks and her mouth. He didn't dare settle into a real kiss because his beard would scratch like the very devil.

"I've known you could be," she said breathlessly. "I've known it forever."

"Turns out you were right." He moved down her body, nipping at her soft skin but always careful not to rub his prickly chin against her. He licked her navel until she squealed and swatted him away.

Then he settled between her thighs, but before he zeroed in on his target, he carefully laid sections of the top sheet over her creamy skin.

"Now that's crazy." She lifted up to watch what he was doing. "I don't care about a little whisker burn down there."

"But I do. Now lie back and relax because I'm going to make you come again. It's been at least an hour, so you're due."

She flopped back onto the mattress. "I was wondering when you'd check the schedule and realize that."

"Now. Right now." And he returned to his favorite place in the world. To think until last night he'd never visited paradise. He'd never experienced her seashell-pink softness, moist with her arousal. He'd never tasted the tangy aphrodisiac of her.

And he'd never heard her rich moan of pleasure when he used his tongue right *there*. He circled the spot again and she arched off the bed. He raked her gently with his teeth and she cried out. Then he took full control and she exploded against his tongue, bathing it in all things wonderful.

She was right that he'd gone crazy. Licking and nuzzling her heat in the aftermath of her climax, he was already looking forward to the end of the day when they could be alone and he was granted the right to touch her like this again.

He dared any man who'd discovered this kind of paradise to maintain his sanity. He'd tried to drive her away, but she wouldn't go. Instead she'd moved closer and invited him to enjoy her body for as long as he wished.

God help him, he wasn't strong enough to refuse an invitation like that. She knew all the terrible truths about him and she still wanted him in her bed tonight. And when they came together again, they'd have supplies. He'd finally know what it was like to sink deep into her warmth.

He suspected that sensation would make him crazier than ever.

6

CHELSEA HAD ALWAYS imagined she could tell whether a couple was having sex by the way they acted with each other in public. She thought about that as Finn pulled the gray SUV into a circular gravel drive in front of the Last Chance's imposing log ranch house. Not only had she and Finn spent most of the past twelve hours in bed together, but on the way here they'd made a quick detour to the Shoshone General Store. Consequently a box of condoms rested in a small bag at her feet.

Finn thought the purchase would eventually be common knowledge in a town the size of Shoshone, but Chelsea was okay with that. Or so she told herself. Having people know that she was involved with Finn shouldn't matter. Her nerves were probably due to the presentation she was about to give.

No, that wasn't it. Last night when she'd first met the Chance family, she hadn't been sleeping with Finn. Now she was, and despite considering herself a modern, evolved woman, she felt a little self-conscious about that. Stupid, but there it was.

"The Chance family has quite the layout." Finn braked in front of the steps leading up to an elaborately carved wooden door. Rockers lined the long front porch, which stretched on either side of the main entrance.

He glanced at a parking area off to the side of the house that was already crowded with cars and trucks. "Maybe you should get out here. Might be easier on your shoes."

"It would. Thanks." Besides, if she arrived first, that might emphasize the professional nature of her trip here and minimize her connection with Finn. This was a business event, after all, and she was the one giving the presentation. She'd rather not have anyone speculate on her personal life today.

"I'll help you carry your stuff in."

"That's okay." A truck pulled in behind them and she quickly opened her door and grabbed her laptop case. "You should probably vacate the driveway and get a space before they're all gone."

He hesitated.

"Seriously. Much as I appreciate your offer." He was in gallant cowboy mode and certainly looked the part. She'd had trouble keeping her hands to herself when he'd appeared in a dark blue shirt with silver piping and gray Western slacks that matched his hat. "I can handle this."

"Okay." But he didn't look happy about it. "See you in a minute."

"Okay." She stepped down and wobbled a bit as she made her way across the gravel driveway with her laptop slung over her shoulder. She hoped the gravel wouldn't chew up her heels. They weren't expensive, but she liked them and they went great with this dress.

And now they had a hot memory attached. She'd never forget the sensation of Finn gently removing her shoes. The memory sent warmth rushing through her and she paused on the first step to give herself a quick lecture.

Thoughts that made her skin flush were exactly why people would suspect she was sexually involved with a certain tall cowboy.

Instead of thinking about Finn, she should concentrate on her immediate surroundings. He'd told her that the Last Chance Ranch was considered a landmark around here, and she could see why. Few people built a two-story log house this immense unless they planned to turn it into a hotel.

Fall flowers in yellow and orange bloomed in carefully tended beds on either side of the steps, softening the overpowering effect of the massive structure. The square center section was flanked by two wings set at an angle resembling open arms. She couldn't imagine how many square feet the house must contain.

As she mounted the steps, the door opened and Jack Chance came out, dressed like Finn except all in black. "I estimated you'd be arriving about now." He flashed a smile. "Let me carry your laptop." He neatly divested her of it before she could open her mouth.

"Thank you, Jack." Cowboys just couldn't help being chivalrous, apparently. If they were hardwired to make these gestures, she might as well relax and enjoy it.

"Lily's inside setting up the projector."

"Lily?" She started toward the door, although he'd probably get his hand on the handle first.

"She's a computer genius, literally." He moved ahead of her and opened the thick wooden door. "When you asked about a projector and screen, I put Lily on the case. She's married to Regan, Nick's partner in the vet clinic, and she also runs an equine rescue operation on the far side of town." He motioned Chelsea inside the house.

"Equine rescue? That sounds fascinating. I wonder

if she'd be willing to do some guest lectures at Thunder Mountain Academy."

"You should ask her. She'd probably love it if you took a drive out there tomorrow to see her setup."

"Great idea." The possibility of adding an equine rescue expert to the staff was exciting, both from a humanitarian and a marketing standpoint. She prayed that many generous backers awaited her inside so that all the plans could go forward.

Inside the entryway she took a quick inventory of the living room, which was already full of people. A magnificent curved staircase swept up to the second floor and a wagon-wheel chandelier hung from the beamed ceiling. She figured the usual furniture had been moved elsewhere. Instead, straight-backed chairs and a few folding ones had been lined up in front of the fireplace, which had been draped with a white sheet.

No one was sitting, though. They'd gathered in groups around the perimeter of the room to chat with friends and neighbors. Everyone clutched either a mug or a glass and most held a small plate of cookies, too.

A long table on the left side of the room was the source of the goodies. A coffee urn sat there, along with a clear glass dispenser for lemonade. Platters of cookies were on the far end, along with plates and napkins.

As a PR person, Chelsea was delighted with the welcoming venue. As a staunch supporter of Thunder Mountain Academy, she was touched. Thank goodness she'd spent so much time on her presentation and felt good about how it would be received.

Sarah hurried toward her and held out both hands. "Chelsea!"

"This is such a wonderful thing for you to do, Sarah."

Chelsea squeezed her hands. "It sets just the right tone for the presentation. Thank you."

"It was a group effort. I can't wait for you to meet everyone, but I'm sure you'll want to check with Lily first. She's right up front with Jack."

Chelsea turned and discovered Jack had taken her computer case with him. He stood next to a card table while he talked with a woman wearing jeans and a tie-dyed shirt. She also had the reddest hair Chelsea had ever seen. Gabe's wife Morgan had red hair, but this woman's was so bright it practically gave off sparks.

"Come on." Sarah motioned Chelsea to follow her. "You can trust Lily. She'll make sure the technical part of your presentation goes off without a hitch."

"Great." She made her way up the aisle behind Sarah and was introduced to Lily. Chelsea liked her firm handshake and her steady, intelligent gaze. "I appreciate you being here."

"Of course! I would have showed up anyway, so I'm happy to help."

Sarah squeezed Chelsea's shoulder. "I need to go mingle. When you're finished setting up, come on over to the refreshments table and I'll introduce you to a few people."

"Perfect. Thanks." Chelsea sent her a look of gratitude.

After Sarah left, Jack glanced at Lily and Chelsea. "All set, then?"

Lily smiled at him. "Chelsea and I have everything under control. Thanks for helping me bring in the projector."

"No worries. Sorry Regan couldn't make it."

"Me, too, but that mare needs him right now." After Jack walked away, she turned back to Chelsea. "My husband's a vet."

"Jack told me."

"He wanted to be here, but he got called out to monitor a problem pregnancy. Jack helped me with the projector. God love these cowboys, they can't stand to see a woman carry anything heavier than a purse."

Chelsea laughed. "I've noticed."

"Anyway, let's get you hooked up and test the system."

As they were setting up, Finn arrived and Chelsea made the introductions. "Lily runs an equine rescue operation," she added.

"Oh, yeah?" Finn looked impressed. "What a great thing to do."

"Isn't it?" Chelsea glanced at Lily. "Would you mind if we came out to see it tomorrow?"

"I'd love to have you. Regan should be there, so you can meet him, too. Come for lunch if you want, although I warn you I'm a vegetarian, so you won't get any meat."

"That's no problem for me," Chelsea said.

"Or me," Finn said. "I'm Wyoming born and bred, so I used to think I had to have steak with every meal, but living in Seattle has changed my mind."

"Then I'll expect you both around one for veggie lasagna." Lily finished hooking up the cables and turned on Chelsea's computer. "Call up your file and let's see if we're ready to rock and roll."

The connection worked perfectly, but Lily insisted on staying to babysit the equipment while Finn and Chelsea went over to join Sarah and be introduced to the guests. Chelsea used her honed memory tricks to keep track of names and faces. That was always good when meeting new people, but it was especially important when asking them for money. She answered questions about Thunder Mountain Academy and explained her involvement in the project.

Finn seemed completely at ease, and she couldn't help

contrasting that to five years ago when she'd worked with him on his own Kickstarter campaign. At first he'd balked at the idea of seeking donations from strangers and she'd thought his reluctance stemmed from being a foster boy. But it had been deeper than that. He'd remembered living with a grandfather who'd never had enough money.

But once he'd understood that renovating the old historic building meant giving something valuable back to the community, he'd gradually become more comfortable with the process. Now he was fighting for the couple who'd created a safe haven for him and so many other boys. He obviously had no problem seeking help under those circumstances.

They made a good team as they chatted with people who might possibly mean the difference between success and failure for Thunder Mountain Academy. The meet-and-greet was going along smoothly until Pam Mulholland arrived. She came over to the refreshments table and smiled at Chelsea and Finn. "So how did you both sleep?"

Finn choked on his coffee, which sent several people, mostly women, rushing to his aid. Chelsea stepped back and let them fuss over him while she ducked her head and tried to regain her composure. If Finn hadn't reacted, she might have been able to keep her cool, but her cheeks felt hot.

Apparently, Jack wasn't one of the people making sure Finn didn't choke to death, because he hurried over to her instead. "Are you okay? You're as red as the paint job on my truck!"

"Thank you, but I'm fine. Just…" What? As she gathered her wits and raised her head to meet his gaze, she scrambled for an explanation that had nothing to do with choking, which would be too coincidental. Finally she sacrificed her professional poise to the cause. "Anxiety attack," she murmured. "I'll be fine once I start my presentation."

"You get nervous?" He didn't seem to be buying it.

"A little."

"Must be more than a little. You really were red."

"I know."

"But you're looking better now. You're more the color of bubble gum than tomato juice." He gave her a wink. "That bright red clashed with your purple hair."

"Lavender." She took a deep breath. "Thank you for being concerned."

He nodded, acknowledging her gratitude, but his dark eyes continued to assess her. Then he lowered his voice. "Funny how you and O'Roarke lost your cool at the same time."

"Life is strange."

"Isn't it? Pam comes in and asked how you slept and O'Roarke chokes while you get stage fright. Go figure."

So he'd guessed what it was all about, but she would neither deny nor confirm. "One of those crazy coincidences."

"I knew when you two walked in the Spirits and Spurs last night you had unfinished business with each other."

"Oh?"

"For what it's worth, I'm in favor of taking care of unfinished business." He patted her on the shoulder. "I should probably also mention that the boys are setting up our little homemade dancing platform for the barbecue tonight. We'll have a DJ instead of live music, but he's an excellent DJ. I can say that because he's Josie's brother. I hope to see you and O'Roarke out there."

"We will be. Last night was fun." Then she realized

that could be taken more than one way. "I mean, the dancing was—"

"I hope it was *all* fun. Now, what do you say? You're the star of this little show. Shall we get this party started?"

She took another deep breath. "Yes."

"You don't really get stage fright, do you?"

"Not really."

"I didn't think so. You're like me, in control of yourself. I don't get it, either. In fact, I'll be up there introducing you, so if you're ready to go…"

"Bring it on."

"Atta girl." Jack cupped her elbow before turning toward Finn. "Showtime, O'Roarke. Everybody else, find a chair!" Then Jack escorted her to the front of the room.

She recognized that his casual gesture of taking her elbow gave her the seal of approval for the entire crowd. If she was Jack's buddy, then they would listen to her. Finn joined her and they stood together as Jack explained who they were and why they were here.

"And as an added enticement," Jack said, "they've brought these amazing Men of Thunder Mountain calendars, created primarily by our own Dominique Chance, who donated her services." He gestured toward where she sat and the group applauded.

"And," Jack continued, "the calendar happens to feature me as Mr. July. Check it out." He opened it to his picture and walked back and forth, displaying it.

Chelsea worked hard to keep from laughing. He was in his element, and he was going to help bring money to the cause. Jack obviously loved his life as a rancher, but if he ever decided to get into PR, he'd be a natural.

"They brought a limited number of these calendars," Jack said, "so if you want to take one home, you have to pledge a minimum amount today. If you donate later on, a calendar will be mailed to you, but what we have here is instant gratification until the supply runs out and the added incentive of autographs from four of the calendar boys. Now, let's all silence our cell phones so we can watch the presentation Chelsea's created for us."

Chelsea gave the signal to Lily and the PowerPoint began. It looked almost flawless and drew generous applause at the end. Chelsea added her pitch for Thunder Mountain Academy, one she'd practiced carefully. She discussed the various items being offered to backers in addition to the calendar, such as weekends at the ranch and guided trail rides. The largest contributions would earn a free two-week session for the teen of their choice.

Then Finn said a few words about what Thunder Mountain Ranch had meant to him and why he felt it should continue teaching the values and skills he'd learned there. He told a few stories that made everybody laugh. But the obvious sincerity in his voice affected everyone, including her.

Afterward Chelsea used the card table as a base of operations, setting up her laptop so guests could make an online pledge. Chelsea's pulse rate jumped as the amount grew rapidly.

She wanted to nudge Finn and get him to look, but he was busy autographing the April page of the calendar. Jack, Gabe and Nick sat nearby, signing their pages, too.

Lily had to take off to check on the animals at her place, but she'd glanced at the screen before she'd left and given Chelsea a thumbs-up. The number kept rising, but at the end, when the last guest had gone out the door, they were not quite there.

Oh, but they were so close. So close. Chelsea was jubilant. She motioned to Finn. "Come see!"

"How'd we do?" He glanced at the screen and whistled. "Not bad!"

That brought the rest of the family over. Amid the hugs, back-slapping and high fives, Finn excused himself to go call Rosie.

When he came back in from the porch, Chelsea walked over to him. "What did she say?"

His voice was husky. "Not a whole lot. Mostly she cried."

"Aww." Chelsea's throat tightened.

"She said to give you a big hug, but if I did that, I might not be able to let you go."

"Later."

"Yeah." He glanced over her shoulder. "Hey, there, Jack."

He came up beside her. "Just wondered how your folks reacted to the news."

"I only talked to Rosie, but she's overjoyed and very grateful. And so am I. This was an awesome event."

Jack rubbed his chin. "The thing is, you've almost got it. I was hoping you'd top out. I'm thinking I should just—"

"No, Jack." Chelsea shook her head. "We still have a few days and you've already been so generous."

"She's right," Finn said. "Much as I'd love to hit that magic number today, we're so damn close. That money's bound to come in. You hosted this event and made a sizable pledge already. Someone else will come through for the rest."

"All righty, but if that needle is still sitting there on the last day, you call me, you hear?"

"We will," Finn said. "Don't worry. But I'd say we've got it." His smile was a mile wide as he gazed at Chelsea. "We've got it."

"Well, in that case, let's celebrate!" Jack turned and spread his arms wide. "It's time to party, but first we have us a little mess to deal with." He started folding up chairs.

Chelsea immediately stood and folded up her chair.

"Whoa, not you, Miss Chelsea." Jack came over and took the chair. "You're our honored guest. Only the family has to work around here. And O'Roarke can lend a hand, because I know how much he'd hate being forced to sit and watch us slave away."

She looked him in the eye. "So would I, Jack. Thanks for giving me a pass, but I intend to do my share."

"Oh, well, in that case, here." Grinning, he handed back the chair. "Welcome to the family."

7

FINN COULDN'T BELIEVE the transformation in Chelsea during the past few hours. She'd morphed from a polished professional who made all the right moves, kept track of names and said all the appropriate things, to a goofy lady who joked around and didn't seem the least bit worried about her appearance.

When the air turned cooler during happy hour out on the porch, Sarah took her inside to raid her closet. Chelsea returned looking like a kid in her big sister's clothes. She'd rolled up the legs of the too-long jeans and the sleeves of the oversize sweater. Amazingly, the shoes fit.

As everyone commented approvingly on her outfit, she paraded up and down the porch like a model on a runway. Later on, Josie's brother Alex and his wife, Tyler, arrived with all the grandkids in tow. Nick and Dominique's son Lester, a teenager they'd adopted several years ago, developed an instant crush on Chelsea.

Finn could completely relate to the kid's starry-eyed worship. Chelsea took it in stride and teamed up with Lester to direct the smaller kids in a game of hide-and-seek until it was dinnertime. Naturally all the kids wanted to sit with her, which meant Finn was out of luck.

During the meal served outside, she ate barbecue with her fingers and then licked them clean. It was cute as hell, but it was also erotic. He finally had to stop watching.

Instead he talked with Alex and Tyler. Alex was blond like his sister Josie while Tyler had dark hair and an olive complexion. Cassidy had a date, so Uncle Alex and Aunt Tyler had volunteered to watch all the kids for the afternoon.

"And I'm not too proud to admit I'm bushed." Alex grinned. "They're great kids, lots of fun, but, oh, my God, are they active."

"Thank heaven Chelsea was willing to take over when we got here," Tyler said. "I love them to death, but I was so ready to turn them over to somebody else. I don't know how Morgan does it with three under the age of five."

"And Morgan's your sister, right?" Finn was still trying to keep everyone straight. He didn't have Chelsea's skill at matching names and faces.

"I know it's confusing," Tyler said. "I took after our Italian mother and Morgan took after our Irish father, so nobody can believe we're sisters, but you can tell immediately that Alex and Josie are related."

"I can." Finn glanced at Alex. "Your sister has a great venue in Shoshone with Spirits and Spurs. I envy her that antique bar with the mirrors and brass fittings. I'd love to have something like that in O'Roarke's, but it wasn't in the budget."

"Josie was smart," Alex said. "She bought it when the market was down and the owners wanted out. Now Spirits and Spurs is a little gold mine." He smiled. "She wants me to help market her beer once she gets going."

"You're in marketing? I thought you were a DJ."

"Only for Chance parties now. I handle the marketing for the Last Chance's horse-breeding program."

"Does Chelsea know that? I'll bet she'd like to trade war stories."

"She might not know." Alex gestured to the table where Chelsea was wiping the barbecue from a toddler's face. "She threw herself into the breach right after we got here and we didn't have a chance to talk. In fact, I wish we could have been here to see the presentation, but babysitting seemed more important."

"Next time Cassidy has a date," Tyler said, "I might have to fly Chelsea in from Seattle."

"I had no idea she was so good with kids." Finn watched the action at the other table with admiration.

"How long have you been together?"

He swung back to Tyler in confusion. "Excuse me?"

Her eyes widened. "Whoops. Sorry. I just assumed… never mind. I shouldn't have leaped to conclusions. Bad habit."

"No need to apologize." Finn took a steadying breath. "We've worked together for five years but never dated. Recently…" *Less than twenty-four hours ago.* "That's changed."

Tyler nodded. "I'm glad my radar isn't totally off. She seems very special."

"She is." He glanced over at the table and noticed that Josie, Morgan and Dominique had descended and were claiming their respective offspring. "And I think she's just been relieved of duty. Excuse me a minute." He moved toward her but hung back as she hugged each tearful child in turn.

Josie passed by first, holding her son Archie by the hand and carrying her daughter Nell. "We're giving the kids a bath and putting them to bed in the ranch house," she said. "I told Chelsea how much we appreciate her effort, but please mention it again. She was a lifesaver."

"I'll tell her."

The five younger ones all left, but Lester seemed reluctant to go. Dominique talked to him, and at last he nodded and trudged back to the house with her.

Chelsea came toward Finn, her smile bright as the stars blinking overhead. "Hi."

"Hi, yourself. When you said I had a lot to learn about you, you weren't kidding."

"I love kids. My cousins all have kids and I'm constantly volunteering to watch them. They're so creative and uninhibited. And the parents seem to love having a break."

"You amaze me." He'd never seen her like this, in clothes that didn't fit and her lipstick worn off. A little girl's flowered barrette was in her hair, probably lovingly placed there by one of the girls. "A few hours ago you were the consummate professional."

She shrugged. "That's one side of me."

"You do realize Lester is smitten."

"He's adorable. Dominique promised him that if he'd help get the other kids in bed, he could come back and have one dance with me."

"Just one?"

"That's all. Dominique explained that I already have a boyfriend, but that you'd allow him to have a dance with me because you're a nice guy."

Finn's pulse rate kicked up a notch. "I suppose she just said that because she needed to keep Lester from getting too attached."

"No, she said that because everyone here assumes we're sleeping together."

That sent his pulse into overdrive. "Why?"

"The way you look at me. The way I look at you. I thought maybe it wouldn't be obvious, but Jack picked up on it this afternoon when we both freaked out about Pam's comment. Judging from things other people have said to me, it's now everybody's assumption that we're together."

"And yet we haven't even had sex yet, not really. Not in the classic sense of the word."

She looked into his eyes. "But we will."

"Oh, yeah." He was suddenly short of breath. "I'm ready to leave now, but we can't."

"Nope. Not after they went all-out for us. We need to stay and celebrate." Her eyes shone. "But I was just thinking that we're close enough to the goal that I could put the rest on my credit card."

"No, that's not a good—"

"I won't do it now. That's only if we get down to the wire. I'm not letting this get away when we're inches from the finish line."

"Let me talk to Damon and Cade. They might have some room on their cards. You shouldn't be putting it on yours when you've already done so much."

"I'm sure none of us will have to worry. The money will come in. But I'm just saying that it's within range and I really don't want to call Jack."

"I know. We're close enough now that we can figure it out among ourselves. And, boy, do I feel like celebrating…in private."

"We will. Be patient."

"I'll do my level best, ma'am." He lowered his voice. "While you were licking barbecue sauce off your fingers, I thought I might have to excuse myself and take a cold shower."

She smiled. "Exactly what I was going for."

"Chels."

"What? Is there some rule that you can't take care of little kids and taunt your lover at the same time?"

"Honest to God, if we didn't have to stay here, I'd haul you back to the B and B and—"

"Hold that thought." She touched her finger to his lips. "Now let's go over and talk to Alex and Tyler. I heard he's in PR and she's the event planner for the town. They might have some suggestions for Thunder Mountain Academy."

His brain still fizzing with thoughts of barbecue sauce and Chelsea's naked body, he followed her back to the table where Alex and Tyler were sitting. If he'd worried that she'd abandon all thoughts of their project now that the presentation was over, he was dead wrong. She might not be dressed to impress, but she obviously wouldn't let that stop her from making important professional contacts.

"We didn't get to talk before." She sat beside Tyler. "But I didn't want to miss a chance to pick your brains. Has Jack filled you in on what we're doing at the academy?"

"He did," Tyler said, "but before we get into that, thank you from the bottom of my heart for taking over entertaining the kids."

"It was fun. I've had lots of practice with my cousins' kids."

"You'd think I'd had lots of practice coming from a family of seven, but I've forgotten what I ever knew about children, apparently."

"And I never knew much in the first place." Alex shook his head. "It's embarrassing to admit I can be intimidated by a five-year-old, but I'm no match for Sarah Bianca."

Chelsea laughed. "Oh, yeah, SB. She informed me that

she's going to be a saddle maker when she grows up. I guess she met Ben Radcliffe when he delivered Sarah's birthday saddle last December and she's decided that's the job for her."

"Too bad she's not a little older," Finn said. "She could enroll in the academy."

"It'll still be there when she's sixteen." Chelsea said it with conviction. "That's only eleven years from now. I love thinking of the long-range possibilities of this program."

"That's the strength of it," Alex said. "I've built the Last Chance campaigns on longevity. The academy is new, but the history behind it isn't. I'm sure you used that in your presentation."

"She did." Finn was eager to share the finer points of the video. "She got clips from my foster mom that showed the contribution to the community that Thunder Mountain has made in the past and then she connected that to the potential for continuing that kind of legacy. It was great."

"Send us a copy," Tyler said. "I have a few contacts from my days as a cruise director. If you don't mind, I'll share it with them and see if they might have grandchildren who would be interested in the program, especially if grandma and grandpa were willing to finance it."

Chelsea beamed. "That would be awesome. The more people who know about it, the better."

"Have you considered radio spots for future marketing?" Alex pushed away his empty plate. "People still listen to the radio in their cars. I don't know what your advertising budget will be once you get everything in place, but I could check out some of the major markets and get back to you. If you decide to go that route, I'll record a spot for you."

"Fantastic idea!" Chelsea beamed at him. "I'll look forward to getting the info. Anything else?"

"The calendar's great." Tyler sipped on her wine. "Fun intro. But once you have things rolling, how about doing another one featuring a special student for each month? You'd have to get a release from the parents or guardians, but I think—"

"Yes!" Chelsea bounced in her chair. "Brilliant. Parents would go nuts over that. After today's success, we can start seriously planning for that in the future. I love that idea."

Alex gazed at her. "Anytime you want to brainstorm, just call, email or text."

"I will. I wish I'd known earlier that the Chances had both a marketing guru and an event planner in the family."

"My job's pretty easy," Alex said. "The horses practically sell themselves, plus you've seen Jack in action. He schmoozes like nobody's business. And then we'll have Gabe put on a cutting-horse demonstration, and people can't get their money out fast enough."

Chelsea sat up straighter. "Cutting-horse demonstration?" She glanced at Finn. "Did you know about this?"

"Nope, but I can see where you're going with it."

She turned back to Alex. "Do you think he'd consider teaching a session here and there at the academy? He'd get paid, of course. We don't expect any of the instructors to work for free."

"I can't speak for him, but I think he'd love it." He turned to Tyler. "Don't you?"

"I do. He used to enter competitions all the time, but he doesn't do that as much now that he has three kids. A few teaching gigs might be just the thing—a short trip without the stress, yet he'd have a reason to keep his skills sharp."

"Then I'll ask him."

"Ask who what?" Jack came up to the table.

"Gabe," Tyler said. "Don't you think he'd love teaching cutting-horse sessions at the academy?"

"Hell, yes. Sounds perfect. The competitive circuit was too intense for a family man, but now he's bored and driving Morgan crazy."

Tyler laughed. "I didn't want to say that, but it's the truth." She glanced at Chelsea. "You'd be doing both Gabe and my sister a big favor."

"Yep," Jack said. "I recommend you broach the subject tonight. He'll be here any minute. The kiddos are almost tucked in. We're about ready to start the dancing if our friend Alex here will stir his stumps and spin us some tunes."

"I'm on it." Alex pushed back his chair. "I expect all of you to get out on the dance floor and make this effort worthwhile."

"We will, sweetie." Tyler smiled at him.

Finn experienced a moment of panic when he thought he might be expected to alternately escort Tyler and Chelsea onto the floor. He decided to take defensive action. "I should warn you, Tyler, that I'm not a very good dancer."

"Relax, Finn." She reached over and patted his arm. "The word's out already."

"It is? Who talked?"

"Shoshone's a small town."

He sighed. "I didn't realize it was *that* small."

"Well, it is. Everyone knows everyone else's business. Apparently, Jack gave you enough of the basics last night that you can manage, but Jack, Gabe, Nick and even Pete will make sure I enjoy a few dances. It's not your job."

"Thank you."

She smiled. "You're welcome."

He turned to Chelsea, about to ask her for the first dance, when Lester appeared at her elbow.

His gaze was filled with adoration. "Mom said I could ask you to dance, but only one time. So would you like to?" He shot a furtive glance at Finn. "That's if it's okay with your boyfriend."

Finn regarded him solemnly. "Chelsea makes her own decisions."

"I'd be honored to dance with you, Lester." The music hadn't started, but Chelsea rose from her chair and walked with Lester to the wooden dancing platform. Lester was short for his age, so without her heels, Chelsea was about his size.

Alex's voice came on the mike. "It's a beautiful night in Wyoming. Let's rock and roll!" And the music blasted out, something loud and full of energy.

Lester looked startled, but then he began gyrating to the beat. Chelsea did, too, and in her borrowed clothes, she looked more Lester's age than her own. Considering her lack of dancing experience, she did a fair job of it.

Other couples quickly joined them. Finn spotted Jack and Josie, and they weren't dancing the two-step. Instead they looked like a couple of teenagers wiggling around up there.

"Alex is from Chicago," Tyler said, "so he'll play country songs most of the time, but he's known for throwing in some classic rock to shake things up."

"Looks like everyone's good with that."

"They are. And Lester's having the time of his life."

"Yeah." Finn couldn't help grinning as he watched Chelsea rocking out. "So's Chelsea."

"She's great. I don't know either of you very well yet,

but I hope this works out between you two. You seem right for each other."

"Thank you." Finn didn't know what else to say. And suddenly he didn't want to be on the sidelines anymore. "Listen, you don't have to go up there with me, but would you like to dance?"

"Sure. Why not?"

So he escorted Tyler to the dance floor. Turned out she was a woman with rhythm to spare. She coaxed him to let go, and he found himself rotating his hips in ways he'd never tried before. He finished the dance laughing and breathless. When he looked for Chelsea, he found her gazing at him with a knowing smile.

After giving Lester a hug, she walked over and glanced at Tyler. "Can I borrow him for a while?"

"You bet. I got him all warmed up for you."

"Much obliged." Chelsea grabbed him by the shirtfront and tugged him to the center of the platform. "Dance with me, you sexy cowboy."

As a slow country tune started up, he pulled her close and gazed down at her. "You know, if anybody had any doubt…"

"They don't. Do you mind?"

"Nope."

"Good." She slid her arms around his neck. "Without my heels, we don't match up quite as well."

"Sure we do." He nestled her head against his chest and wrapped his arms around her as he swayed to the beat and moved as little as possible.

"Are you doing that shuffle thing?"

"I am." He rested his cheek on the top of her head. She sighed. "Nice."

"Uh-huh." He'd never felt so warm and alive, or so

sure that he belonged right here with Chelsea at this moment in time. Thunder Mountain Ranch was about to be saved. For now, everything was perfect.

8

ALTHOUGH CHELSEA WOULDN'T have minded going straight from the dance floor back to the Bunk and Grub, that wouldn't be a very polite way to end the evening. So she and Finn stayed, and while she desperately wanted to be alone with his adorable self, she had a good time dancing and hanging out with the Chance family.

When they drove away a couple of hours later, after she'd changed back into her clothes and hugged everyone goodbye, she almost hated to leave. Then she glanced at the strong profile of the Stetson-wearing man behind the wheel of the SUV, and she didn't mind leaving at all.

He looked over at her. "I feel like it's been years since I kissed you."

"Same here."

"Hang on. This'll be a fast trip."

"Better not push it. Remember what Alex said."

"About what?" He hit a rut hard and swore under his breath.

"You need to go slower."

"I can see that, but you'd think they'd do something about this damn road."

"I guess you were getting us drinks when Alex and Jack were talking about that. It's bumpy on purpose."

"You're kidding." He hit another rut, but at this speed they only bounced a little.

"Sarah's first husband liked keeping the surface rough. He thought it discouraged trespassers. After he died, Jack declared it would stay that way. They only grade it when it gets *really* bad."

"Then I suggest they get out here with a tractor, because it's *really* bad."

"Alex was trying to convince Jack that it was time, but Jack just laughed. Apparently the debate over the road has been going on for years."

"Well, it's worse at night, that's for sure. When we drove in, I probably avoided the ruts without thinking much about it. But it's black as pitch out here. I'll have to crawl."

"Probably a good idea."

"It's a terrible idea." He eased over to the side of the road and switched off the motor. Then he put his hat on the dash.

"Finn, what are you doing?"

"Something I've been thinking about for hours." He unfastened his seat belt and opened his door. Reaching up, he turned off the overhead light.

That simple gesture told her what he had in mind and her pulse switched into high gear.

Moving with deliberate purpose, he walked around to her side of the SUV and opened her door and the back door. Next he deftly released her seat belt. Last of all he picked up the bag from the floor and put it on her lap. "Hold these." Then he scooped her up in his arms.

"You can't be serious!" Her heart pounded in anticipation. "Someone could come along!" Despite that protest, her skin heated and moisture gathered between her thighs.

"No, they won't. They all decided to stay for poker. Nobody will be on this road for another two hours."

"You're certifiable." The night air did little to cool her off. Finn was taking charge and she was on fire. "Totally insane." Yet as he leaned down to tuck her inside the backseat of the SUV, she helped him by scooting across the smooth leather.

"We already knew that." He unbuckled his belt, stripped it off and tossed it on the floor. "Now it's just a question of degree." He reached for the button on his jeans.

Her breath caught. He hadn't asked. He hadn't suggested. He'd simply taken command of the situation, and now she was wild for him, so wild that she felt as if she could come at any second. "Stopping alongside the road to have sex when there's a perfectly good bed waiting definitely puts you higher up on the scale." The paper bag rattled when she took out the box. She was trembling just that much.

Nearby, crickets chirped in the tall grass. It was the only sound except for the distinctive buzz of his zipper. "I'll take one of those."

He was only a dim outline in the darkness, but she handed a packet toward him and he plucked it from her fingers. "You'd better take off your panties." His voice was thick with desire. "I might rip them."

She tugged them off over her shoes, not bothering to unbuckle those little straps. He wanted her *now*. God, that was exciting.

Tossing the damp panties to the floor, she hitched up her dress. No time to take that off, either, because he was climbing in.

"Scoot down a little." The words came out tight with strain. "There." Strong hands slid along her thighs, parting them, positioning her, finding her moist entrance. "Ah, Chelsea. You're so wet."

She gulped for air. "Because...I want you."

"I'm here." Braced above her, he slowly guided the blunt tip of his penis into her slick channel. "So good." He gasped. "So damned good."

She had no words. The sensation of him filling her left her speechless and quivering with pleasure. Instinctively she clutched his beautifully firm ass and urged him forward.

He groaned and plunged deep. She came at once, arching upward with a sharp cry. Breathing hard, he remained rock-solid, firmly tucked inside her as he absorbed her contractions. When they slowed, he began to pump.

Immediately her body tightened again. She would always treasure what they'd shared the night before, but this...*this*. She whimpered with the glory of it, reveled in the sensual feel of his muscles bunching and releasing as he stroked.

At first he moved easily, but soon his thrusts became faster, until at last he drove into her with relentless precision. Her second climax lifted her off the seat. Wailing, she gasped out his name.

Bracing her backside with one large hand, he held her there as he sucked in air and pushed in tight. His powerful orgasm vibrated through her and his full-throated groan of satisfaction shattered the stillness of the night air. Then, slowly, he lowered her to the smooth seat and followed her down. His cock continued a slow, rhythmic pulsing, sending delicious shock waves through her body.

He gulped for air. "My God. I had...no concept."

"No." She panted, unable to catch her breath. "Me, either."

"I feel like someone hit me with a sledgehammer."

"Then don't move."

His soft chuckle seemed to increase the intimacy of the moment. "I can't. Not yet."

As she lay beneath him, waiting for the world to settle down again, she realized that neither of them would ever forget this. Had they driven back to the Bunk and Grub first, the experience certainly would have been memorable. But it wouldn't have been nearly as vivid as coupling in the backseat of a rented SUV under cover of a cool and very dark Wyoming night.

"Are you okay?"

She laughed. "Never better."

"So I didn't mash you against the seat or bang your head against the armrest?"

"No. You just gave me two mega climaxes in a row and probably wrinkled my dress." Then she considered her right shoe, which was currently pressed against his thigh. "Is my high heel hurting you?"

"I can feel it, but it's kind of kinky to think of us doing it while you wore your shoes."

"Finn O'Roarke, I do believe you're a sensualist."

"Takes one to know one. Where's your mouth?" He finally located it with the tips of his fingers. "I need to kiss you."

"Okay." She waited until his lips found hers. Then she cupped his head and kissed him back.

"Mmm." He slipped his tongue into her mouth.

She sucked on it gently and felt his cock twitch.

He lifted his mouth away from hers. "Okay, guess we can't kiss, after all. This has been fun, but I want the next time to be in an actual bed."

"Not up against the wall?"

"How you talk!" He gave her a quick kiss and began slowly easing away from her. "Yeah, maybe up against the wall, now that you mention it. I checked, and Pam is staying with Emmett tonight so we'll have the main part of the house to ourselves again."

"Maybe she's doing that on purpose to give us privacy." She groped around for her panties.

"Maybe." He climbed out of the SUV.

As she found her panties, which were unsurprisingly damp, she could hear the rustle of material as he put himself back together. "I'm not putting my panties back on, FYI."

"Are you telling me you're going to ride back to the Bunk and Grub commando?" He zipped his pants.

"Yes, I'm telling you that."

"You do realize I'll be thinking about it the whole way there." He grabbed his belt and threaded it through the loops.

"Now I do. Bonus."

"You're a wicked lady, Chelsea Trask."

"Apparently you find that appealing."

"I think I just demonstrated how appealing I find that. Okay, scoot over here and I'll carry you back to the front seat."

"I'll scoot over, but you don't have to carry me. I can walk."

"There's high grass and loose dirt. Not the kind of terrain for those sandals. Let me be a hero."

"You already are, but okay." She slid toward the door. "Ready."

He leaned in, but instead of picking her up, he kissed her. Not only that, he slipped his hand under her dress and fondled her until she was squirming. When he backed away she was once again breathing hard.

She swallowed. "No fair."

"Oh, it's very fair." He scooped her into his arms and carried her around the open door before settling her in the front passenger seat. "Girls who announce they're going commando, which makes the guy's cock hard as a gearshift while he's trying to drive, have to expect a little payback. Now buckle up."

He really had her motor running, now, and she loved it. They'd settled into a sexual give-and-take that was exactly how she'd imagined it might be with Finn, only better.

He climbed behind the wheel, closed the door and fastened his seat belt. "What did you do with your panties, by the way?"

"They're on the floor back there along with the box of condoms. Why? Looking for a souvenir?"

"I won't need one." He started the car and pulled back onto the road. Then he reached for her hand. "I'll never forget that episode."

"Neither will I."

He laced his fingers through hers. "Thank you, ma'am. I appreciate you indulging me."

She smiled at his deliberate cowboy-like expression. "Like you gave me a choice."

"I didn't, did I? But somehow I had a feeling you'd go for it."

"Then you're starting to know me better."

"Good. That's very good." He released her hand and took a deep breath. "Now let's talk about something safe so I'm not compelled to pull over again and do you."

And he would, too. Her body grew moist and hot. "Like what?"

"I want to know how you can be totally focused on work one minute and then it's like you flip a switch and you're able to play hide-and-seek with a bunch of kids."

"You mean how do I separate work and play?"

"Yes. Because obviously I can't. I've been able to let go this weekend because I'm far away from O'Roarke's and there's not much I can handle from here."

She hesitated. It was an important question that could impact both of them. "I think it's something you could learn," she said carefully. "If you wanted to."

"I'm not so sure. When I'm in Seattle, I have a constant need to check inventory, taste-test the brews, monitor the cash flow...just *be* there."

"Kind of like the parents of a newborn."

"I know nothing about that, but, yeah, maybe."

"I've watched my cousins, and they were all like that with their first kid."

"And then they got over it?"

"Eventually. It took some longer than others. The second kids are always easier."

"Well, I'm not opening a second brewhouse. That would make me twice as anal." He was quiet for a while. "I don't think it's the same, though. Kids grow up to be self-sufficient, or at least that's the plan. A business never learns to run itself."

"No, but you can delegate some of the work."

"Um, yeah. I'm trying not to imagine how Brad is doing without me there. When I was gone in June I came back to a total mix-up with receipts that took a week to straighten out. It wasn't anything that would sink the ship but, face it, he's not as invested as I am." He took a deep breath. "Let's talk about your family some more."

She could feel the tension radiating from him, so she gladly changed topics. "I have a younger sister, but I felt as if I had more siblings because my aunts and uncles were usually around with their kids."

"In Seattle?"

"No, in Bellingham. That's where my folks live and where I went to high school and college."

"See, I didn't even know where your hometown was. I thought it was Seattle."

"It is now. I think of Seattle as home." She paused. "Do you?"

He hesitated. "I think so. But after the divorce… I haven't felt like my cramped little apartment is home. It still feels temporary."

"It probably is temporary. Where would you live if you could afford any place in Seattle?"

"Somewhere down by the water, within walking distance of Pike Place Market and O'Roarke's. Something like what you have."

She told herself not to put any importance on that. "Then you should focus on what you want. You'll recover from the financial hit of the divorce and eventually you'll be able to live down there. I may be renting now, but I plan to buy when I feel comfortable taking on that kind of obligation."

"And you'll do it. You always accomplish what you set your mind to."

"Not always." She'd been so convinced that his divorce was divine intervention and they were destined to be together. But even now, when they'd had such great sex, she wasn't sure. The explosive nature of that sex might be the very thing that would scare him off. He had a business to run.

They rode in silence for a few minutes and she wondered if he knew what she was thinking. He might.

If so, he obviously didn't want to talk about it. "What do your folks do in Bellingham?"

"Both college professors. Mom's in psychology and Dad's in economics."

"And you didn't want to follow in their footsteps?"

"God, no. My sister, Beth, is getting her graduate degree, but I don't have the patience to teach the same bunch of students for an entire semester. My folks love it, but I would go postal if I had to walk into the same classroom three days a week. I like more variety than that, more control over my schedule. I was born to be self-employed."

Finn laughed, and the tension seemed gone. "I was, too. My grandpa couldn't get it right, but I knew that was the life for me. His bad example taught me a lot about what not to do."

"And in a twisted sort of way, he helped you."

"I suppose. Rosie tried to get me to see that, but at the time I wasn't willing to listen. I was a self-righteous kid who thought I'd never make any big mistakes. Boy, was I wrong."

She reached over and squeezed his thigh. "Give yourself a break, O'Roarke. We all mess up eventually."

"You don't."

"Sure I do." She let her hand rest there because she loved feeling his thigh muscles flex as he worked the gas pedal.

Without warning, he captured her hand and held it against his thigh. Then he slowly moved it to his crotch. "Feel that?"

Did she ever. His fly barely contained what lay beneath. "Yes."

"That's what happens when you put your warm hand on my thigh. All I can think about is finding the nearest flat surface—horizontal or vertical, doesn't matter—and pounding into you until neither of us can see straight."

"Sounds fun." She was being flip but her heart beat like a jackhammer.

"Oh, I'm sure it will be. But you'd better keep your hands to yourself or I'm liable to seduce you in the parking lot of the Bunk and Grub." He pressed her hand tight against his fly and then gently placed it on the console.

She sat there quivering and wondering if she could last until they reached the parking lot, or if she'd end up begging him to pull over again and take her now, right now. She'd never been this crazed with lust for a man. That made her vulnerable, and she briefly acknowledged that. But with the prospect of having Finn in her bed all night, she couldn't bring herself to care.

9

FINN WAS PLAYING with fire and he knew it. The deeper he allowed himself to sink into this sensual bliss with Chelsea, the more difficulty he'd have extracting himself when the time came. And it would come. On this trip he felt free to carve out large sections of time for this madness, especially now that Thunder Mountain was as good as safe. Back in Seattle it would be a different story.

But he would challenge any man to turn his back on a woman who sashayed up the dimly lit stairs of the bed-and-breakfast in strappy sandals, a dress wrinkled from backseat sex and no panties. The irresistible aroma of sex trailed after her, and his cock swelled with every step leading to the room where he could have her again.

At her suggestion, her laptop had stayed in the locked SUV. He smiled thinking about her terse *"Leave it."* She was as eager for him as he was for her, which almost convinced him to reach for her and take her on the stairs. No one was around and he had a box of condoms in his hand.

He controlled himself. He'd already given in to his impulses once tonight in the backseat of the SUV. Surely he could wait five more minutes before he turned loose the primitive urges raging through him.

He clenched his jaw as she fumbled with her key. Knowing that she fumbled because she was shaking with anticipation only inflamed him more.

The night before he'd held back, asked questions. All that was gone now. Once she opened the door, they tumbled inside, each of them wrenching at the other's clothes. Maybe because she'd planted the idea, he did take her up against the wall, her legs locked around his hips and her breasts jiggling with every firm thrust.

The rhythm was muted but steady. If anybody had been close by they would have known exactly what was going on in this room. He felt her tighten, felt his own orgasm surge forward and shoved deep. They both came, their cries mingling as their bodies trembled and throbbed.

He sagged against her, gasping, his head spinning as he rested it on her shoulder. He couldn't say how long they stayed like that. After a rocket-ship ride with Chelsea, reentry was a slow process.

"Finn." Her breath tickled his ear.

"I know. We need to move. Give me another minute."

"It's not just that."

He dragged in a breath and raised his head to look into her eyes. "What?"

"We left the door open."

He turned to see, and sure enough, her bedroom door stood wide-open. If anyone had been around and had cared to peek in, they would have enjoyed an eyeful. "Oh."

She snorted with laughter. "Is that all you have to say? *Oh?*"

"Well, yeah." He grinned at her. "I mean, what sort of comment covers a situation like this? We just had wall-banging sex with the door wide-open to the hall of this very lovely bed-and-breakfast. What would the etiquette police say about that?"

"They might suggest that we close the door. Even though we're fairly sure no one is upstairs at this hour of the night, we could be wrong. The housekeeper might have heard strange thumping noises and come up to investigate."

"If she works in a bed-and-breakfast and thinks rhythmic thumping noises at eleven on a Saturday night are strange, then she's lived a very sheltered life."

"I agree, but we should still close the door."

"You're right." He let her down slowly so she wouldn't fall. "I'll leave that to you while I take care of the condom."

"I should be able to manage it."

When he returned, she'd closed the door and climbed into bed. But she'd thrown back the covers so that he was treated to the sight of a naked Chelsea stretched out on soft white sheets. Another woman might have covered herself, but not Chelsea. She apparently liked the no-holds-barred dynamic they had going on.

And so did he. He probably liked it way too much, but now was not the time to question that. All he had to do was to gaze at her lying in bed propped up by several snowy pillows, and he felt desire stir in his groin.

She watched him approach and her glance moved from his face to his slowly rising cock. "Again?"

"That's just my opinion. You may be getting sick of this."

She looked up at him. "Finn, I'm going to tell you something, and maybe it's a mistake, but I'll tell you anyway."

"What's that?"

"From the moment I first saw you in that coffee shop, I've dreamed about having sex with you."

He found that hard to believe. She'd been so sure of herself, and he'd been so clueless about how to survive in the big city. "Why?"

She smiled. "Just asking that question, for example. You're incredibly good-looking but you don't seem to realize it. Women notice you, but you don't seem to see them noticing."

"Sometimes I do."

"You don't act like it."

"If I notice back, then that implies I might want to start something. And I have a business to run." He heard himself and groaned. "God, that sounds sanctimonious. I promise to stop saying that. Even I realize it's becoming obnoxious, like I'm the only person in the world with responsibilities."

"But you're the sole owner of that business," she said gently. "And that's another thing that attracted me. You're very brave. Not too many guys I know would move by themselves to a distant city and plan to open a business on their own."

"And I would have crashed and burned if I hadn't met you."

"I don't think so. It might have taken you longer to succeed, but you were extremely focused."

"Still am."

"I get that. But as you said, the business is far, far away." She patted a spot next to her. "And I'm right here."

He picked up the box of condoms from the floor and tossed them in her direction.

Catching it neatly in one hand, she rolled to her side, facing him as he climbed in beside her. She placed the open box between them on the mattress. "Two down, ten to go."

"Should've bought a bigger box." He took one out and laid it on her pillow. "But first, I'm running low on kisses." Closing the box, he tossed it over his shoulder and it landed...somewhere. He'd find it later.

For the moment his primary target was her rosy, plump mouth. The brief thought that all this kissing might have to end someday made him even more eager to taste often and well. He moved over her and supported himself on his elbows while he gazed into her eyes.

Reaching between them, she wrapped her fingers around his cock. "I want this." Her eyes darkened as she stroked him.

"And you'll get that, but now it's kissing time. Turn me loose so I can concentrate."

"You're getting bossy." But she released him and slid both hands up to his shoulders. "This better be a really good kiss."

"You tell me." He stroked the pad of his finger gently over her lower lip. Leaning down, he nibbled on it before tracing it with the tip of his tongue.

"That tickles."

"I love touching you here." He outlined the graceful bow of her upper lip with his finger and then with his tongue. "Your mouth is perfect for kissing. Like this." He pressed his lips to hers briefly, lightly, playfully. "And this." Changing angles, he did it again. "And this, and this, and this." He kept it up until she laughed.

"You're silly."

"Mmm." Then he captured her mouth fully, fitting it to his with deliberate intent. He made a leisurely exploration with his tongue, sliding it easily along hers.

Her breath caught.

Shifting the angle, he cupped her jaw and stroked the corner of her mouth with his thumb, urging her to open to him. He kept his thumb there and took the kiss deeper. The thrust of his tongue grew more demanding, more suggestive.

She whimpered and hollowed her cheeks, sucking him in. Her fingertips dug into his shoulders as she lifted into his kiss, her mouth hot and eager. He responded with firm strokes that told her exactly what would happen next.

As she moaned and arched her body toward his, silently begging for that next step, he barely restrained himself from taking it. Ending the kiss, he grabbed the condom, tore open the package with his teeth, and rolled it on.

She lay there gasping. "Hurry."

"Oh, yes, ma'am." He sank into her slick heat with a groan of pleasure. Then he looked into her passion-dark eyes. "This part of you is perfect, too." He pushed deep.

She took a shaky breath. "That was one hell of a kiss."

"You helped make it that way." He eased back and slid in up to the hilt again.

"It was so close to…this." She wound her legs around his, cinching them even closer together.

"My plan." He dipped his head and took her mouth again as he held himself still inside her. Only his tongue moved, yet she tightened around him as if he'd been thrusting steadily.

One spasm became two and then she was coming, sucking hard on his tongue as her climax rippled over his cock.

His climax followed quickly, urgent and strong, making his toes curl and his body flush with heat. He lifted his mouth away and gulped for air. Then he leaned his forehead against hers. Gradually his heartbeat returned to normal.

"Some kiss, O'Roarke." She slowly relaxed and sighe in obvious contentment. Her breathing evened out.

When he roused himself enough to look into her eyes again, they were closed. "Chels?"

She didn't respond, although a smile remained on that beautiful mouth. She'd fallen asleep.

How like her to go until she couldn't anymore. She hadn't wanted to give up these precious moments any more than he had. But finally exhaustion had claimed her.

He gazed at her with a rush of tenderness laced with guilt. She'd been a willing partner the night before and she'd given her all today despite not getting a full night's sleep. After a successful presentation and the triumph of almost reaching their goal, she'd entertained five young children and danced for two hours. Then she'd once again become his enthusiastic lover.

Dropping a light kiss on her forehead, he eased away from her. "Sweet dreams, Chelsea Trask."

SHE WOKE TO golden light streaming in the window and no Finn in bed with her. But he'd left a note on Bunk and Grub stationery propped on the nightstand where she'd see it right away.

Dearest Chels,
I decided to sleep in my own room because if I
stayed here, I might reach for you in the night.
Maybe you wanted to have sex with me from that
first day we met, which is still amazing to me. But
I doubt you wanted to have this much sex. I'll see
you down at breakfast.
Yours,
Finn
PS I put the condoms in the nightstand drawer.

She thought back to the last thing she remembered from their night together. He'd kissed her so thoroughly that he'd created an intense craving. He'd proceeded to satisfy that craving by locking them together and kissing her again until they'd both had an orgasm without moving at all. Incredible.

After that…she had no idea. Apparently she'd fallen asleep with his cock deep inside her. But he didn't sound insulted in his note—his words were sweet and considerate, just as he was when he wasn't being macho and sexy, or adorable and funny, or…preoccupied and anal.

She showered and dressed while she thought about that last aspect of Finn O'Roarke. It had the power to cancel out all the rest. She'd witnessed it first-hand during the painful episode when she'd asked him out and he'd calmly explained why he couldn't accept.

He might well be someone who wasn't capable of delegating because he didn't trust anyone else to do the job. If that was the case, then he wouldn't have room in his life for her or any woman. He could build a successful business in Seattle and expand the territory for his microbrewery. Someday he'd have the money to buy a place down near the water.

She'd continue to get her checks for a percentage of his booming business, but she wouldn't be in the picture otherwise. Ironically, he could make her a lot of money. She'd rather have the man than the money, but she might not get that choice.

His door was open when she walked into the hall a little past eight. She checked to see if he was in there, but the room was empty. He'd pulled up the covers on his bed, although she wouldn't say he'd actually made it. His laptop was out and his gray hat was brim side up on the dresser.

The signs of his solitary life made her sad, as if he'd already moved on. He hadn't, of course. They were scheduled to spend many more days together, and she couldn't imagine him giving up sex with her unless she was the one who called a halt.

She wouldn't do that. Right now he clung stubbornly to his world view, and maybe he was right. But there was always the chance that he was shortchanging himself. In that case, she'd be there when he figured it out. If he never figured it out, she'd have some beautiful memories of what Finn was like unplugged.

Pam had been right—the smell of coffee led her straight back to the breakfast room. It turned out to be a sunny spot filled with green plants and several tables and chairs that reminded her of outdoor cafes in Paris. She'd never been to Paris, but she'd seen enough pictures to recognize the look.

Finn sat alone at a table drinking coffee and reading a newspaper. He'd turned back the sleeves on his long-sleeved white shirt to reveal his muscled arms sprinkled with dark hair. That alone was enough to tighten the coil of desire in her belly.

He must have heard her footsteps because he glanced up. His smile of welcome told her that he had no intention of pulling back from their interlude. He stood and watched her approach. "You look ready to visit an equine rescue operation."

"It's the best I can do." She'd worn a long-sleeved purple T-shirt, jeans and her running shoes.

"You look great." His gaze moved over her with a trace of hunger.

"Thanks." She cherished that hunger because she wasn't sure whether he'd look at her that way once they were back in Seattle.

"How did you sleep?"

"Like the dead." She lowered her voice. "Missed you, though."

"I didn't trust myself." He motioned to a chair. "Have a seat. I'll get you some coffee. I asked Yvonne to hold off breakfast until you showed up." He walked over to a coffee urn on a side table.

"What if I'd slept until ten?"

He had his back to her as he filled her cup. He shrugged. "We would have made different plans."

"You could have gone ahead and eaten."

"No, ma'am." Turning back to her, he brought her coffee and set it in front of her. "That's not how I operate."

"Meaning what?"

He sat across from her. "Meaning that I want to share breakfast with you."

She looked into the warmth of his blue eyes. "That's nice, Finn. I'm sorry I fell asleep on you last night."

He shook his head. "I'm the one who should apologize. I don't know what I was thinking. I knew you were concerned about the presentation and had stayed up late working on it before the flight. Then I kept you up the next night with…"

"I wanted that as much as you," she said softly.

"I know, but yesterday was intense with the presentation, convincing backers to contribute, and then playing with the kids, and then dancing. I didn't think about you being tired. I just thought about—well, you know what I thought about."

"I thought about it, too. You still don't seem to realize how much I crave your—"

"There she is—the sleeping beauty!" A small, dark-haired woman came into the room. "Are you ready for breakfast, now, Miss Trask?"

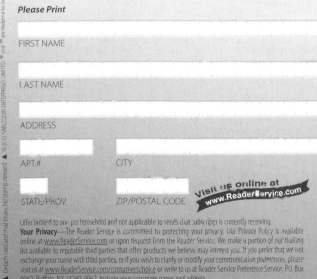

Send For
2 FREE BOOKS
Today!

I accept your offer!

Please send me two
free novels and two mystery
gifts (gifts worth about $10).
I understand that these books
are completely free—even
the shipping and handling will
be paid—and I am under no
obligation to purchase anything,
ever, as explained on the back
of this card.

150/350 HDL GJAQ

Please Print

FIRST NAME

LAST NAME

ADDRESS

APT.#   CITY

STATE/PROV.   ZIP/POSTAL CODE

Visit us online at
www.ReaderService.com

"I'm starving," Chelsea said. "Are you Yvonne?"

"I am, indeed."

"And you cook as well as handle the housekeeping chores?"

"That's right." She smiled. "It's a beautiful house to work in."

"It is! And you make wonderful pastries. I can't wait to have some more."

"Coming right up!" The housekeeper turned and headed back to the kitchen.

Finn's attention remained on Chelsea, almost as if they hadn't been interrupted. "I'm flattered that you want me that much, but you know what? Maybe it's time for me to back off a little and let you catch your breath."

She met his gaze. "Don't you dare."

"All right." He chuckled. "But maybe we should at least have some breakfast first. We need to keep up our strength."

"Of course, if you need me to back off so you can catch your breath, then—" She gulped in surprise as he left his chair and pulled her out of hers.

His mouth came down with deadly accuracy. His kiss was short but it delivered a powerful message that left her gasping. Then he settled her back in her chair and returned to his. "Does that answer your question?"

"Yes." She took a shaky breath. "I do believe it does."

10

KISSING CHELSEA MIGHT not have been the wisest course of action. Finn no longer cared about breakfast. He wanted to haul her back upstairs. But he couldn't forget the moment when he'd glanced down and discovered that she was fast asleep. When she was awake, she was a force to be reckoned with, a woman with a sharp wit and a smart mouth.

But with her eyes closed and her mouth curved in a soft smile, she'd looked...vulnerable. She didn't need a man to protect her. He'd never make the mistake of assuming that. She was totally in charge of herself and would resent someone who suggested otherwise. He wouldn't back off, but there was nothing wrong with slowing down, just a little.

So after Yvonne served the food, they ate a leisurely breakfast. They had things to discuss, after all, concerning Thunder Mountain Academy—Gabe's potential classes in training a cutting horse, Alex and Tyler's suggestions, and Lily as a potential guest lecturer on equine rescue efforts.

When they'd finished eating, they lingered over coffee. Now that they'd become lovers, it was a totally different experience from the old days when they'd met in the coffee shop to go over business issues. Without the constant level of sexual frustration that had made all their Seattle discussions edgy and vaguely uncomfortable, they could relax and just be with each other.

"It's so good to know the end is in sight and, one way or another, we'll have the money by the deadline," Finn said.

"No kidding. I'm glad it won't be like that nail-biter we had with yours."

"That was intense." They'd hovered over her computer in the same coffee shop where they'd met and reached the goal a few minutes before midnight. Then they'd gone out for drinks.

She smiled. "That might be the only time I allowed myself to drink too much when I was around you."

"Same here." He met her gaze. "I almost asked you to come home with me."

"I almost asked you to come home with me. But I was afraid you'd say no."

He sighed and leaned back in his chair. "I might have. I don't know. I was pretty happy that night and we'd had several rounds. I might have said yes."

"And then regretted it in the morning?"

He hesitated as he considered the question. "At this point, I can't imagine ever regretting being with you, but, yeah, it's possible. Honestly, Chels, I don't know why you haven't written me off."

"I tried, especially when you married Alison. I worked really hard to find someone who'd take my mind off you."

"I know." Even now his chest tightened when he remembered those agonizing months of his marriage and Chelsea dating other guys.

"No, you don't. You didn't even notice."

"How could I not notice? You brought that first dude, the one with the pretentious beard, into O'Roarke's."

"He did not have a pretentious beard."

"Oh, come on. Trimmed to a little point? Give me an effing break."

"Okay." She seemed to be trying to keep from laughing. "It was pretentious. And scratchy."

"I don't want to hear about that part. All I know is you cuddled in a booth with him for an hour and forty-five minutes."

"You timed us?"

"Damn straight. Watched the whole sickening performance from the kitchen and every minute was torture. Don't tell me you didn't bring him in on purpose so you could wave him in front of my nose."

"Of course I did! But you never said anything so I thought you hadn't seen us and it was a wasted effort. And don't talk to me about torture. You were *married*."

"Dear God." He scrubbed a hand over his face. "Well, we won't be going through that kind of nonsense anymore. I'd say our cards are finally on the table."

"But the game's not over."

"Yes it is." He reached for her hand. "No more games. I love being with you and wish I could be more like you so that I could neatly compartmentalize my life. I don't know that I can."

She gave his hand a squeeze. "I believe you can, but that doesn't matter. *You* have to believe it."

"I wish I could." Looking into her eyes was a pleasure, one he'd denied himself for years. He hadn't dared let his attention rest there, but now he took every opportunity to bask in the warmth of her gaze. "I'm glad we're going to Thunder Mountain. It seems really important for you to see it."

"I can't wait, Finn. I've been hearing about the ranch ever since we met and I know how much it means to you. I wouldn't miss going there for anything, especially now that we know Rosie and Herb will be able to keep it."

"I'd like to leave first thing in the morning, if that's okay. We can grab breakfast here, but then take off."

"Works for me. Are you willing to drive again?"

"I thought I would. Then you can look at the scenery. You didn't do much of that on the drive from the airport."

"Actually, I could use those hours to work."

"Oh." He shifted his thinking. "Are you getting behind? Here I've been raving on about taking time away from my job and you've had to do that, too."

"No worries. It's just that right before we left I picked up a new client. He knows I had this trip, but he'd like to have a proposal for his new PR campaign ASAP. He's on a tight deadline and if I can come through, he could be a good source of income for future campaigns."

Her comment provided a much-needed reality check. "Then definitely I'll drive and you can work. I should have asked you before if you had your own stuff to do instead of assuming you were going to be fancy-free once the presentation was over." He released her hand and pulled out his phone. "We don't have to leave for Lily and Regan's until a little before one, so you'd have some time now if you need it."

She shook her head. "It's a beautiful day. I'd rather take a walk through town. Shoshone's so different from what I'm used to and I'd like to check it out. Who knows when we'll be back?"

"Sounds great to me, but I don't want to interfere with whatever you need to do."

"I promise you won't. I wanted to make this trip, both to help out and to be with you. I'll do some work tomorrow, and maybe a little bit while we're at Thunder Mountain. It'll be fine."

Once again, she seemed so comfortable with switching back and forth between work and play, so certain nothing would fall between the cracks. He envied the hell out of that. "Then I'll get my hat. Need anything from upstairs?"

"Just you."

Damn, but that sounded nice. "Be right back."

"I'll wait for you on the front porch."

"Okay." He whistled a catchy little tune as he made a quick trip upstairs. They'd danced to it the night before, although he couldn't remember the lyrics. He hadn't whistled in years...five, to be exact.

What an uptight bastard he'd become. Now that the tension was ebbing away, he'd like it to stay gone. But would it? He knew himself, and once he was back in Seattle, he'd probably have the same compulsion to monitor everything 24/7. Although this trip had given him some breathing room, the fear of failure still lurked in his heart.

After fetching his hat, he went out onto the front porch and found Chelsea sitting in a white wicker chair looking as mellow as he felt. She had a project demanding her attention, but she was putting it aside to spend time with him. He didn't take that lightly.

"You look settled in," he said. "Would you rather stay on the porch and watch the world go by?"

"I'm not sure a lot of the world will go by on this little corner." She stood. "Let's go explore."

"Yes, ma'am." He held out his hand and she linked her fingers through his without hesitation. Walking along the sidewalk holding hands seemed so natural, yet they'd never done it before.

He'd kept any touching to a minimum with Chelsea.

Oddly enough, she'd done the same, although she was a hugger with people she knew and liked. He decided to mention it. "I just realized that until this weekend, you've never hugged me."

"That's right."

"So it was intentional, then. Did you think I'd push you away?"

"I wasn't sure what you'd do, but I decided not to risk it, considering the heat we seemed to generate when we were close to each other. I figured a hug could go one of two ways. Either you'd reject it because it was too intense, or we'd end up in the nearest coat closet tearing at each other's clothes."

"Option B is the most likely. I touched you as little as possible because I didn't trust myself. I was worried about that on this trip." He laughed. "Guess we know how that turned out."

"Blame it on the dancing."

"Or I could drop to my knees in gratitude because of the dancing, and the cold walk home, and finding myself in the room next to yours with no other guests in the house."

"So you don't think you'll regret what's happened?"

"I'd be a fool if I did." He hesitated. "How about you?"

"To steal your comment, I'd be a fool if I did."

"No matter what?"

She squeezed his hand. "No matter what. Obviously you believe we won't have the same dynamic in Seattle, and you could be right."

"I probably am. I've known myself a long time."

"True, but we won't find out until we get there. At least we won't have that other thing, that weird Frankenship where we couldn't admit we were in lust."

"*'Frankenship'?*"

"Sort of a friendship, but with strong sexual overtones that made us act like zombies around each other. A Frankenship. It's a term I made up."

He grinned. "Perfect description. I'm glad we killed it."

"Actually, you killed it. I was headed into my room to sleep alone Friday night until you admitted you were crazy for me."

"But then I was ready to give up for lack of condoms. I say killing our Frankenship was a combined effort. And now it's dead." He took a deep breath. "And I've never felt more alive."

"Good sex can have that effect."

"It's not only the sex, although that's a huge part of why I'm feeling so good. It's—I hate to say this—it's being away from O'Roarke's."

"But weren't you gone for almost a week in June?"

"Yeah, but I was worried sick about Rosie, and then when her condition seemed to be less dire than we'd all thought, we found out that they were about to lose the ranch. Now Rosie's in good health and we have a way to save the ranch." He looked over at her. "But mostly it's the sex."

She laughed. "Thought so. Well, we've walked the length of Main Street."

"So we have."

"Now what?"

He paused to look around. "I got so carried away with what we were talking about I didn't pay attention. Sure is quiet."

"Sure is. Except for the diner, everything's closed up tight. A lot different from Seattle on a Sunday morning."

"That's for certain." He glanced back at the area they'd already covered. While engrossed in their conversation, he'd walked past the general store where they'd bought the condoms, a post office, a hair salon and an ice cream parlor, all closed.

Spirits and Spurs stood at the far end on the opposite side of the street. Beside it was a feed store, and he pointed to a life-size plastic horse on its roof. "You won't see anything like that in Seattle."

"Probably not." She glanced at the building next to it. "No one-story banks, either. But judging from the brick they used, it was probably put up about the same time as the building you renovated for O'Roarke's. In fact, there's mostly brick construction along this street, except for Spirits and Spurs."

"Which might be the oldest structure in town."

"I wouldn't be surprised." She gazed across the road where six pickups were angle-parked in front of the diner. "I'd love to support the local economy, but I'm stuffed from breakfast."

"Me, too. We could go there for dinner."

"Oh, I forgot to tell you. Josie wondered if we'd meet her and Jack for dinner at Spirits and Spurs."

He pictured dancing with Chelsea again and the idea filled him with pleasure. "Sure, that would be great."

"She's really serious about a microbrewery and wants to start ordering equipment. She'd love your advice."

"I'd be happy to talk to her about it, but that might not be so easy if there's a band."

"No band tonight."

"Oh."

She chuckled. "You should see your face. Do you want to dance? Maybe they have a jukebox or a sound system."

"I never thought I'd look forward to dancing, but the minute you mentioned Spirits and Spurs, that was my first thought. I do like it way better than I expected to, and besides, it's a great excuse to hold you."

"Then we'll see if they have music available. Ready to walk back?"

"Guess so." He surveyed the street again. "Let's cross over and walk down the other side."

"Watch out for traffic." Then she laughed. "Kidding."

"It really is a sleepy little town." Other than the pick-ups in front of the diner, the street was deserted. "I wonder if Josie can make a go of a microbrewery in a place this small."

"If that's all she had to work with, probably not, but she's planning to draw from surrounding areas, and specifically Jackson. Tyler and Alex have all kinds of promotional ideas once Josie gets going."

"And it'll have the Chance name attached. That should help." He decided the joy of holding hands was underestimated. Feeling that connection while walking with Chelsea was turning into one of his favorite things.

"I don't think she intends to trade on the Chance name. The Spirits and Spurs is her baby, not Jack's, and I get the impression she wants the microbrewery to be her project, too."

"But wouldn't the Chance name boost sales? They're so well known around here."

"It might, and naturally some people will know she's married to a Chance, but she doesn't want to emphasize that. The important hook will be the historic saloon, ghost drinkers in the bar and all of that. This family is terrific, but she doesn't want to be totally defined by her association with it."

Finn had a tough time imagining being overwhelmed by family or rejecting a great marketing tool like the Chance name. "I don't really get it, but my buddy Cade might. He was freaked out when he suddenly discovered he was a Chance cousin and instead of having no relatives he had a boatload. But I was a little jealous of the guy."

"Having been here for a few days, I can see how the Chances could be intimidating. We're dealing with a dynasty here, and Josie wants something that she made all by herself. I can understand that."

"Yeah, maybe. I only had one relative, and that didn't feel like enough."

"But he focused all his attention on you. I had a friend who was an only child and I thought that was great. No competition."

"I guess that's true." He felt an unexpected tug of nostalgia. "We did stuff, just the two of us. Simple things like going fishing and camping, sometimes renting movies if it was bargain day. I need to remember that."

She glanced at him. "He sounds like a nice man."

"He was." He didn't say anything for a while. "I'm kind of hard on him, but he was a nice man. He knew I was lonely. He used to say that he'd love to adopt a sister or a brother for me, but he couldn't afford it."

"That's touching."

"It is now. At the time I was mad because I didn't have anybody to play with."

She squeezed his hand. "I get that. Beth and I have had our knock-down, drag-out fights, but I'm glad she's there. If I ever have kids, I'd like to have two."

"Do you want some, then?"

"I do, assuming I find the right person. How about you?"

He sighed. "Honestly, I don't see myself having any."

"How can you be so sure?" Her words had an uncharacteristic edge to them, as if she might be tired of hearing him say things like that.

"I'm just being realistic, Chels."

She sighed. "I know. Sorry. God knows people shouldn't have children unless they really want them."

"Or feel they can give them the time they'll need."

"Right."

"You'd make a wonderful mother, though."

She glanced at him. "Thank you. I think I would, too."

11

THEY WENT BACK in silence. Chelsea resisted the urge to challenge Finn's stubborn belief that he couldn't be a successful businessman and have a personal life. She hadn't walked in his shoes, after all. She hadn't been a kid whose grandfather had begged for half-priced pastries.

His marriage to Alison hadn't helped matters, apparently. Chelsea hadn't gotten to know her very well. She'd been too busy being pea green with envy. But she suspected that Alison had painted an appealing picture of a more relaxed lifestyle. It was a worthy goal, but Alison hadn't been the right woman to carry it off.

Chelsea had done some investigating after Finn and Alison's quickie Las Vegas wedding. Okay, a *lot* of investigating. Alison worked a nine-to-five salaried job for a paper-products company and she'd met Finn because he placed orders through her.

The life of a business owner had nothing in common with a salaried employee. Someone with a regular paycheck was unlikely to relate to things Chelsea felt on a gut level—the uncertainty of monthly or yearly income, the constant threat of some catastrophe wiping out profits and the realization that you were the driving force behind it all.

She understood why Finn was so determined not to let anything interrupt his concentration. She also realized that if he didn't find a way to deal with that kind of pressure and give himself permission to enjoy life outside of work, he could be headed for a lonely life at best and an early grave at worst.

In her PR business, she'd seen it happen. Whether or not Finn ended up with her, she didn't want him to be alone and unhappy. Someone like Alison wasn't likely to be the answer, as he'd found out. Chelsea couldn't guarantee that she'd be any better at helping him balance his priorities, but she felt qualified to make the attempt.

They exchanged only pleasantries as they returned to their respective rooms and got ready for lunch with Lily and Regan. Chelsea decided pleasantries weren't working for her. Leaving her room ten minutes before they were scheduled to start downstairs, she knocked on his open door.

He glanced up from the room's small antique desk where he'd been typing something on his laptop. "Is it time to go? I thought we had—"

"We do. We don't have to leave yet. May I come in?"

"Sure." He shut down the computer and stood. "Something on your mind?"

"You know there is. We started out that walk in a cheerful mood and somehow ended it on a sour note. I want to fix that."

He tunneled his fingers through his glossy, dark hair, mussing it in a very sexy way. "Me, too. What happened?"

His innocent question grabbed her by the heart. He

wanted to be happy and carefree, but the poor guy didn't know how. "I think we forgot to live in the here and now."

After a long pause he nodded. "You're right. Instead of walking down Main Street and enjoying the beautiful day and a chance to be together, we got into the subject of having kids."

"Yep. A loaded subject that had nothing to do with our activities today. I can't speak for you, but creating a baby is not a high priority for me today. In fact, I was present when we bought an entire box of supplies to keep that from happening."

"So we did." His frown disappeared and a slow smile touched his beautiful mouth. "And that's where we should place our focus, on the use of the contents of that box."

"That's my conclusion." She moved in close and slipped her arms around his neck. "Not right this minute, because we have places to go and people to see. We also have a dinner date with Josie and Jack. But after that…" She wiggled against him.

He pulled her in tight. "And we should take advantage of the privacy we have now because I have no idea how things will shake out for us at Thunder Mountain."

"Because they think of us as platonic business associates?"

"Uh, not exactly."

"What do you mean *not exactly*?"

"I mean that Cade, Lexi and Damon, because they all know me so well, might have picked up on a certain… interest I had in you back in June when we asked for your help."

She was delighted to find out that his friends had some advance knowledge of the situation. "What about Rosie and Herb? Do they have any clue that we might be more than friends?"

"Herb doesn't usually get into that kind of issue if he can help it, but Rosie is a matchmaker from the get-go. She'd love to think something was going on between us."

"But we'll have separate sleeping quarters, obviously."

"I'd expect that. They'll probably give you a room in the house and I'll be out in the Thunder Mountain Brotherhood cabin."

"The cabin you shared with Cade and Damon when you all lived at the ranch?"

"That's it. Rosie always assumes any of us who show up will want to sleep out there for old times' sake."

"Then we'll be separated every night, huh?"

He cupped her bottom and his fingers flexed against the denim. "'Fraid so. Unless we get creative."

"Let's do that." She nudged his fly. "Let's definitely do that."

"It makes no sense for me to sneak into the house where Rosie and Herb would be right down the hall, so you'd have to sneak out and visit me in the cabin."

"How soundly do they sleep?"

"Herb sleeps like the dead. After years of having so many teenage boys to worry about, Rosie keeps one ear open all the time. And she has eyes in the back of her head."

"Maybe that's just as well." Chelsea gazed up at him. "I don't feel right sneaking out of the house when I'm a guest. I'm sure the etiquette police wouldn't approve."

"I figured that would be the case. As it happens, I've given this some thought."

"Have you, now?"

His blue eyes sparkled. "After the past two nights, you think I wouldn't?"

"I'm glad, because I have no clue about this place. I didn't know if we'd have bedrooms right next to each other, like here, but if your foster parents are close by, that's not such a great setup, either."

"That's why I think, all things considered, we should plan on daytime sex."

"Oh, really? Rather than have me sneak out under cover of darkness, you want to do it in broad daylight? Where, pray tell? In the hayloft? In an empty stall? That doesn't sound like a better option to me."

"Cade and Lexi had some hot times in the tack room, but I won't put you through that. Now that I know you can ride, we can pack a lunch, pack our condoms and have us a picnic in some secluded spot."

"Oh." The image of that was erotic enough to dampen her panties. "I've never done it outside."

"It's a whole new experience."

"So you've done it?" She didn't enjoy the image of him enjoying sex in the great outdoors with someone else, but doubtless a guy as cute as Finn hadn't been celibate prior to his arrival in Seattle.

"I have, but it's been a while and I guarantee none of them were as beautiful as you will be lying on a blanket in the sunlight."

"*None* of them? Sounds like you had a high old time in the woods, O'Roarke."

"Hey, weren't you the person who just told me to focus on the here and now? Unless you want me to start asking questions about the guys you've been with…" He lifted his eyebrows.

"No, you're absolutely right. No dwelling on the past or the future. But concerning our present, won't Rosie and Herb suspect what we're doing?"

"Herb won't because I'm sure he feels it's none of his business. Rosie believes everything to do with her boys is her business, but if she likes you, she'll offer to pack the sandwiches and send us on our way."

"*If* she likes me? What if she doesn't?"

"She'll love you. I didn't mean it like that. You're great, and besides, you're the mastermind who helped us create the Kickstarter campaign. Like I said, she'll be trying to play matchmaker."

Chelsea's conscience pricked her. "I don't want to lead her to believe we're headed for the altar, though. That wouldn't be right."

"I'll handle that."

"By telling her what? That I'm a temporary diversion? That's not any better!"

Finn continued to knead her backside, which was making her hot. "I'll tell her that we're exploring our options."

"If she's as sharp as I think she is, she'll recognize that's a load of BS."

"So would you rather swear off sex while we're there?"

"No! I just don't want to fly under false colors. You say she'll know what's going on during these *picnics.* I'm reading between the lines, but Rosie seems like the kind of person—mother, really—who expects that to lead to something permanent. Am I wrong?"

"No." Finn took a deep breath. "That's what she expects."

"Yet you and I are totally up in the air. We've made no promises. We're just enjoying each other for the time being." She liked the idea of emphasizing that to see if he'd object to the description.

He didn't. "That's right."

"I don't know Rosie yet, but I don't think she's going to like it."

"As I said, we could decide not to have sex while we're there."

"Finn, look me in the eye and tell me you'd be fine with that."

He burst out laughing. "You know I wouldn't, not after the hours we've spent in bed together, not to mention the special episode in the SUV."

"Okay, so what about that? We could take a drive. Would Rosie suspect something then?"

"Rosie will suspect something anytime we make an excuse to go off alone. She spent years raising teenage boys. She's honed her instincts."

Chelsea gazed into his incredibly handsome face. "'Exploring our options'? Is that the line you came up with?"

"It is, but if you can improve on it, please do."

"I can't. Now that you've laid it out for me and I understand we're going into a situation where we want to have no-strings sex and your foster mother would prefer a commitment by the end of the week, then *exploring our options* may be all we can go with. But I can't believe she'll be satisfied with that."

"She won't, but we may be able to hold her off with it, at least for a while. She might not corner either one of us to demand what's really going on."

"She'd do that?"

"Rosie is a force of nature. She would do that and more if she thought it was necessary to secure the happiness of her boys. I don't know if she would commit murder for any of us, but I wouldn't want to test it."

"Wow." Chelsea smiled. "Now I really want to meet this woman. She didn't just take in foster boys. She gathered them into her tiger den and is ready to challenge anyone who would dare hurt them. That's awesome."

"She is awesome. You two will get along."

"Even if you tell her we're only *exploring our options*?"

"Sure, because she'll blame that on me. She knows what I'm like and she'll decide that I'm the one holding up the works." His voice gentled. "She's right."

"Not necessarily." Pride made her speak up. "You're a complicated man. I'm not sure I could deal with you in a relationship."

"Bullshit." He slid his hands up her back and massaged her shoulders. "You've dealt with me for five years and you haven't cracked yet. She'll take one look at you and know that if anyone can deal with me, you can."

That fascinated her. "And you, Finn O'Roarke? How do you stand on that question?"

He hesitated. "I wouldn't wish my demons on anybody, Chels. Truth be told, I think you'd be better off if you walked away."

"Now?"

Emotion flickered in his blue gaze. "No. I'm selfish enough to hope that you'll stick it out through the week. The idea of giving you up now, when I've just begun to really know you, is…a horrible prospect."

"Then don't even contemplate it. I'll stick it out through the week, and we'll tell Rosie we're exploring our options."

"Speaking of exploring, I wish we could do that right now."

"Wouldn't that be lovely?" She eased out of his arms. "But we've promised to visit Lily and Regan and find out about her horse-rescue operation. I think that's important."

"I know it is." He walked over to the dresser and picked up his hat. "Let's go." He put it on and tugged on the brim so it dipped down, shadowing his eyes and making him look sexier than ever.

Damn. He was one hot cowboy. She sighed softly.

He glanced at her in alarm. "What's wrong?"

"Nothing, except when you tug on the brim of your hat, it's like foreplay."

He grinned. "Every cowboy knows that. It's one of the major reasons to wear a hat." He slung an arm over her shoulder and guided her out of the room. "I'll try to work that gesture into my routine a few more times before we turn in for the night."

"Now see, if I know you're doing it on purpose to get me hot, I probably won't react the same way."

He chuckled softly. "Yeah, you will."

CHELSEA DISCOVERED HE was right about that. He took off his hat during lunch with Lily and Regan, which turned out to be a cheerful meal as they talked about Saturday's wildly successful event. But when he settled that hat back on his head for the tour of the property, he relaxed into full cowboy mode.

Besides tugging on the brim, he often stood with his thumbs in his belt loops. He even seemed to walk differently, more of a casual saunter than the brisk stride she was used to in Seattle. A slight drawl had invaded his speech.

Fortunately, Lily and Regan's place was fascinating, which kept Chelsea from spending the entire afternoon trying not to stare at Finn.

Peaceful Kingdom had plenty of stare-worthy qualities, including the color scheme. When they'd first arrived, Lily had been quick to point out that she'd painted the barn pink with turquoise trim and the ranch house orange with green trim.

"I wouldn't have picked these colors, but they're growing on me," her husband Regan had said, his loyalty obvious.

As they left the house after lunch, Chelsea put on her shades, but even they weren't enough to mute the outrageous color combination. Regan was a tolerant man. She felt as if she'd met him before, but that was probably because he was Tyler's twin brother. He, too, had taken after their Italian mother.

Lily led the way over to one of her favorite sections of the property, a pen containing two potbellied pigs. Chelsea had never seen one before except in movies.

"Meet Harley and Wilbur. Harley's the bigger one." Lily gestured toward the pen.

"But they're both huge!" Chelsea peered at them as she quickly adjusted her mental picture. "Aren't potbellied pigs supposed to be little and cute?"

"Sure, when they're babies," Regan said. "There's lots of misinformation about these guys out there. People who buy them don't seem to realize they're getting baby pigs. When they grow and need more room and a big mud pit to wallow in, their owners bail. We've fostered several we've been able to adopt out, but we've kept these two. We're partial to them."

Finn moved closer, obviously interested in the creatures. "I always wanted a pig, and I would have named him Wilbur, too." He crouched so he was on a level with them. "You are mighty fine-looking animals."

"If you still want a pig," Lily said, "I'm sure another one will show up here. The word is out."

"No place to keep one in Seattle." Finn stood. "But I've always thought they were cool. I tried to get Rosie and Herb to go for the idea of a pet pig, but they weren't enthusiastic, considering we already had six horses, two ranch dogs and three barn cats."

"I'd never been around pigs until I met Lily," Regan said. "Now I'm a fan. They're fun, affectionate and clean except when they've been rolling in the mud. Maybe your foster parents just need a chance to find out more about them. Lily could probably convince them in no time."

"And that's a great lead-in to what we wanted to ask Lily." Chelsea turned to her. "Would you be interested in doing some guest lectures for Thunder Mountain Academy about the horse-rescue movement? You'd be paid, of course."

Lily's freckled face lit up. "I would definitely be interested! What a fabulous idea, to educate teenagers. I'm amazed I didn't suggest it myself."

"Well, good, that's settled." Chelsea smiled at Finn. "We landed another one."

"And I can talk to your foster parents about pigs while I'm there," Lily said to Finn.

"Or not." Finn laughed. "I was the one who wanted them, and I'll only be a casual visitor. I can't in good conscience push the idea."

"But from what I saw on Chelsea's PowerPoint yesterday, it would be a great place for a couple of these guys." Lily obviously was warming to her subject. "I met Cade and Lexi when they were here. I could see them getting into pigs. Now I wish I'd invited them out to meet Harley and Wilbur."

Regan smiled and put an arm around her shoulders. "I hate to break this to you, but not everybody is passionate about pigs. And the academy's supposed to be about horses, right?"

"Right. But what's wrong with adding a pig or two?" Lily glanced at Finn. "It's worth a shot, don't you think?"

He shrugged. "If you can convince someone that a pig would be a welcome addition, then go for it. I'll even lay the groundwork when we go over there this week."

"Great!" Lily beamed at him. "Take some pictures on your phone. I made sure they were all cleaned up before you got here, so they're ready for their close-up."

"Why not?" Finn pulled out his phone and Lily let him into the pen.

Chelsea watched with a lump in her throat as Finn interacted with the pigs. He talked to them the entire time he was in there taking pictures—and he took dozens of pictures.

Lily moved closer to Chelsea and spoke in a low voice. "Does he have any animals at home?"

"Not now. His ex got custody of the cat and dog."

"He might not be able to keep a pig, but he needs some animal to love."

"I can see that." She saw so much more, too—a little boy who'd scraped out a meager life with his grandfather only to have the man die and leave him alone at thirteen. He'd been lucky enough to get taken in by Rosie and Herb, but even their love hadn't filled the gaping hole created by his past.

Now he was trying to fill it by creating a successful business. She understood why he believed that would be enough. But after watching him with Wilbur and Harley, she knew he needed so much more. She hoped he'd figure that out.

12

THE PIGS HAD been an unexpected bonus and Finn had enjoyed the heck out of them. He'd had a good time touring the pink-and-turquoise barn and meeting the rescued horses, but Wilbur and Harley had been the highlight of the trip. There was no way he could imagine having one in Seattle, though, unless he moved to the suburbs and accepted a long commute to work.

By the time he and Chelsea left Peaceful Kingdom, it was almost time to meet Josie and Jack for dinner. He glanced over at Chelsea. "Unless you want to call and say we'll be a little late, we need to drive straight over to Spirits and Spurs instead of stopping back at the Bunk and Grub."

"We can go straight there. That's fine."

"Those pigs were something."

"They were." Chelsea was quiet for a moment. "Taking a wild guess here, but did you get hooked on *Charlotte's Web* when you were a kid?"

"Yep. My grandfather and I watched the movie on bargain day. The next bargain day I begged him to rent it again, so we did. I kept that up until he said that was enough and we needed to get a different movie. So then

I found the book in the library. I checked it out so many times that one day I came in and the librarian handed me my own copy to keep. I still have it."

"It was one of my favorites, too."

"My grandfather didn't like it. He said it was too sad. But I loved it. To this day I can't kill a spider." He looked over at her. "Even Cade and Damon don't know that, so I'd appreciate it if you'd keep it to yourself."

"Of course I will. I'm honored that you trust me enough to tell me. Besides, I can't kill them, either. I put them in a jar and take them outside. But being soft on spiders is easier when you're a girl."

"I suppose it is." He turned down the road leading to town. "Herb and Rosie aren't going to want to deal with a pet pig. I have no right to try to convince them they should."

"What about Cade and Damon, or even Lexi? Maybe one of them is a fan of the story and always secretly wanted one."

"If Cade or Damon is, they would have backed me on my campaign when we lived there. Lexi might like the story, although I've never heard her mention it. I need to get over this and not expect someone else to adopt the pig I can't have."

"Or you can find out if there's a potbellied pig rescue group in Seattle. You could have a charity event at O'Roarke's to raise money for it."

"Damn, Chels, that's brilliant. Let's do it."

"You want me to coordinate it for you?"

"Who else? Nobody's better at these things than you are. Name your price."

"No price. I'll do it for the pigs. For Wilbur."

About that time he pulled into the parking lot of Spirits and Spurs. He shut off the engine and unlatched his seat belt. Then he laid his hat on the dashboard. "Lean over here. I have an urgent need to kiss you."

She unfastened her seat belt and turned into his out-stretched arms. "We don't have time to stay out here and smooch, you know."

"I know. But I can't last another two or three hours." He cupped the back of her head and felt the silky texture of her hair against his palm. "One kiss. That's all."

"Yes, but how long will it last?"

"As long as it needs to." The console was in the way, but he managed to angle his head so he could fit his mouth over hers. Her sigh of pleasure filled him with joy. This wasn't a kiss of unrestrained passion. Instead he simply wanted to let her know how much he treasured her.

He moved his lips gently against hers and slipped his tongue inside her mouth in one easy, unhurried motion. So sweet. So warm. So…oh, God, he was lost. With a groan he took the kiss deeper.

She pulled back, breathing hard. "Finn, we can't—"

"I know. Sorry." And he went back for more.

If she'd pushed him away, he would have abided by her decision, but she didn't. Instead she grabbed the back of his neck and hung on while he plundered her eager mouth.

He wasn't sure how long the tapping at his window had been going on by the time it finally registered. He lifted his mouth from Chelsea's and gulped for air. "Somebody's…outside."

"Oh!" She scrambled away from him and looked over his shoulder. "It's Jack."

"Of course it is." With a sigh he turned to see Jack giving him a Cheshire-cat smile. The windows were automatic, so he had to switch on the power to roll it down. *"What?"*

"Hate to interrupt."

"Sure you do."

"Josie sent me out to see if you were here yet. She's made a small batch of what she hopes will be her signature beer and—"

"Already? I thought she was just thinking about it."

"Oh, no. She's been experimenting for a while, just for the hell of it, not sure if she wanted to do this. Then she saw the calendar and realized you were a brewer. She's been extremely focused ever since. Your glass is poured and she doesn't want it to get warm. This means the world to her, and because I love her dearly, I want you to lay off the tonsil hockey and come in and taste her beer." He smiled again. "If you would be so kind."

"We'll be right there," Chelsea said.

"Excellent. I'll tell her." Jack touched the brim of his black Stetson and walked back into the saloon.

Finn glanced over at Chelsea, who seemed to be trying not to giggle. "He violated the cowboy code, you know."

"He did?"

"Well, not the big, superimportant code, but there's a whole list of lesser infractions, and interrupting a hot kiss is right up there at the top."

"Extenuating circumstances." She flipped down the visor and combed her hair with her fingers.

"Like what?"

"The woman he loves is inside on pins and needles, waiting for your evaluation of her signature beer. He needs you to come in and put an end to her suffering."

"Do you realize what an impossible situation this is? What if I hate her signature beer?"

"You'll find a diplomatic way to suggest improvements."

He dragged in a breath and picked up his hat. "Then let's do this thing."

She grabbed his arm before he could get out. "Whatever you do, don't take a sip and make a face."

"I wouldn't do that. I have some sensitivity."

"You're right. You're the guy who won't kill spiders." She patted his cheek. "I know. Imagine Josie as Charlotte. Instead of working on an amazing web, she's been crafting this beer."

"There are so many things wrong with that image that I don't even know where to start. I'll just have to fumble along on my own."

She climbed out before he could round the SUV and escort her, almost beating him to the front door of the saloon. But he got there in time to open that door, at least. The oval glass inserts were similar to what he'd ordered for O'Roarke's, but these were probably original.

The crowd was thin, probably because there was no live music scheduled. Josie and Jack sat at a far table in the same area where they'd all gathered on Friday night. Probably the designated Chance family corner.

As he and Chelsea approached, Josie gave them a nervous smile and her blue eyes were filled with misgiving. "I thought this would be casual and fun, but I'm rattled." She gestured to the glass of beer sitting in the dead center of the table. "If it's awful, you have to tell me. Don't spare my feelings. This is business."

Finn pulled out a chair for Chelsea before sitting. "I'm sure it's not awful."

"Jack says it's not." She flipped her blond braid behind her back. "But he's required to pump me up. I'm counting on you to tell me the truth."

"I had no idea you'd moved this far into the process."

"I didn't want to say anything because I wasn't sure if I'd have the courage to ask you to taste this. But Jack convinced me that I need to take advantage of you being here. You'll be gone in the morning, so…" She gestured toward the glass. "There it is."

Chelsea spoke up. "Does it have a name?"

"It does if Finn likes it. If he doesn't, then it shall remain nameless and I'll go back to the drawing board."

"No, no, that would be putting too much importance on one person's opinion." Finn prayed the beer would be good. "You shouldn't give my judgment that much weight."

"But you're more of a beer connoisseur than any of us," Josie said. "I'm sure you tasted hundreds of different types before you started brewing your own."

"Yes, ma'am, I did."

"There you go."

"But don't throw out the recipe if I don't like it. We can talk about modifications." Finn decided to lay the groundwork for a potential negative reaction. "Handcrafted beer is tricky. Some brewers work a year or two perfecting their product, some a lot longer than that."

"I know. I've been reading and trying different things. I finally have something I like, but nobody's tasted it except Jack."

Jack waved a hand in the air. "And she doesn't trust my opinion. Go figure. I may not be a brewer, but I've spent a lot of years drinking the stuff and I think—"

Josie clapped a hand over his mouth. "Don't say anything. I want Finn to go into this without any preconceived ideas."

Finn eyed the glass of beer and thought that taking

the first sip wasn't so different from diffusing a bomb. He cautiously reached for the glass.

"Wait." Josie held up both hands. "I forgot to say the most important thing. I don't want you to worry that not liking my beer will somehow jeopardize the Chance family's support of Thunder Mountain Academy. This is completely separate. Right, Jack?"

"Completely separate."

Finn wanted to believe that, but Jack's devotion to Josie was a powerful thing. Anyone who hurt Josie's feelings might not be particularly popular with Jack. Finn was the official representative for TMA, so Jack's good opinion of him seemed pretty damned important.

Once again, he reached for the glass.

"Wait." Josie stopped him again. "I should explain that this beer was crafted with somewhat substandard equipment. That's the other thing I want to talk about tonight. I'm ready to sink some real money into good equipment, so as you taste this, please imagine it being made with whatever you have, because that's what I'm planning to get."

"All right." He had no idea how in the hell he'd make allowances for equipment. The beer either worked or it didn't, but she was a beginner and might not realize that.

He reached for the beer a third time, half expecting that she'd stop him again for another disclaimer. When she didn't, he lifted it to his mouth. He deliberately didn't look at her, but he could feel her tension from across the table.

Closing his eyes, he took a sip. Then another. And one more, just to make sure. Opening his eyes, he smiled at her and put down the glass. "It's great."

With a whoop of joy, she leaped from her chair, overturning it and bumping the table. Jack grabbed the beer before it went over as Finn stood and Josie bear-hugged him. Then she pulled Chelsea out of her chair and hugged her, too. Finally she raced back around the table to give Jack a resounding kiss.

His smile was a mile wide. "We need food," he declared, "and more of this beer, because I happen to know Josie has more of it chilling." He glanced over at Finn with a look of gratitude. "This calls for another celebration."

"I completely agree." Chelsea's face was flushed. "And by the way, is there a jukebox?"

"Sadly, there is not." Josie glanced from Chelsea to Finn. "Are you two turning into dancers, then?"

"Yes, ma'am," Finn said. "And it's all Jack's fault."

"Glad to take the blame."

"You were both a huge help Friday night and now we're excited about dancing." Chelsea settled back in her chair. "But we don't have to have music tonight. I just wondered about the jukebox, because this saloon seems like a natural place for one."

"It is." Josie nodded. "You're not the only one to ask, either. I need to get serious about installing one for the nights we don't have a band."

"Great idea," Jack said. "In the meantime I'll order us up some food. What's everybody ready for?" They gave him their orders and he headed back to the kitchen.

After he left, Josie glanced over at Finn. "So the beer's really okay? You haven't had any more of it."

"I was waiting until everyone had a glass. Sitting here guzzling it all by myself seemed rude."

"But you would have guzzled it?" Josie's expression was endearingly anxious.

"I would. We just need more so we can propose a toast."

Josie's shoulders sagged with relief. "I liked it, and Jack liked it, but I wouldn't let anybody else try it once I knew you'd be here this weekend. Then I lost my nerve and almost didn't ask you. Jack kept pushing me. I'm glad he did."

"Yeah, I'm awesome. Best husband ever." Jack appeared with a tray holding three more glasses.

"Best one I ever had," Josie said with a grin.

"With excellent taste in both women and beer." Jack put down the tray. "Food's coming up soon."

Finn waited until everyone was settled before lifting his glass. "A toast to the Spirits and Spurs signature beer, which is called..." He looked over at Josie.

"Galloping Ghost!" She raised her glass.

"To Galloping Ghost!" they chorused.

Finn touched glasses with everyone, lingering as he clinked with Chelsea's. Funny how he'd thought he couldn't get any closer to her than he had last night. How wrong he'd been.

Sex had knocked down the physical barriers between them, but in spending the day with her, he'd started chipping away at all the mental barriers he'd thrown up to protect himself. And not just from her, either. He'd asked her not to tell his foster brothers that he couldn't kill a spider because of Charlotte.

Why not tell them? They might tease him, but so what? They knew he had that book. He'd kept it on a shelf in the cabin for years. They'd probably figured out that he'd lobbied for a pig because he loved the story of Wilbur and Charlotte.

Watching Josie take this courageous step also made him aware of how self-protective he'd been all his life. She'd let them all know that she was nervous. He would have bluffed his way through the situation by pretending he was totally cool with it. In fact he had done that several times.

Josie put down her beer and reached under her chair. "Before the food comes, I want to ask you about equipment." She pulled out a couple of catalogs he recognized immediately.

Chelsea got up. "Josie, you should switch places with me." She moved over to Josie's seat and Josie sat next to Finn.

From the moment Josie opened the first dog-eared catalog, Finn was rocketed back to the days he used to sit under a large shade tree at Thunder Mountain Ranch, planning his strategy. He'd taken a course on brewing at the community college in Sheridan and he'd worked at a local bar from the moment he was of legal age.

And he'd saved—Lord, how he'd saved, although he'd known in his heart it wasn't near enough. Chelsea had found a way for him to raise the rest. Josie would have more resources than he'd had, but after hearing that she wanted to do this without bringing the Chance family into it, he couldn't assume she had unlimited funds.

So he didn't recommend the top-of-the-line equipment. He didn't have that, after all. Besides, he could honestly give her the pros and cons of what he'd invested in. She'd brought a pen and made notes as they talked.

He lost track of time and even where they were. He did love the process and that was a good thing to remember. Over the years he'd let worry about staying solvent take some of the joy out of doing the work. Josie's excitement brought back what he'd lost.

They'd discussed most of the major items by the time the food arrived.

Josie closed up the catalogs. "That'll get me started."

He pulled out his phone. "Let me send you my email and phone number. You'll have more questions. I sure did."

"I can't thank you enough, Finn." She picked up the catalogs and stood.

"It's been fun."

"For me, too!"

"Hey," Jack said from across the table. "Don't move on our account. Chelsea and me, we've bonded over here. You two can stay put and talk shop. Chelsea's filling me in on the wonders of Seattle. Now I'm hankering to go up in that Space Needle and take me a ferryboat ride."

"You should come and visit," Chelsea said. "It's a beautiful city."

"Then I want to hear about it, too." Josie sat again and tucked the catalogs under her chair. "We've had enough beer talk for the night."

"If you say so. And, oh, will you look at that? Here comes our entertainment, right on time." Jack put his napkin beside his plate and got up to welcome two cowboys who came in carrying guitar cases. "Glad you could make it."

"I'm just sorry our gig in Cheyenne kept us from being here for the barbecue last night." The shorter one, who had a handlebar mustache, shook Jack's hand. "Trey covered himself in glory. I was honored to be on the stage with him."

"Congratulations." Jack grasped the younger man's hand firmly. "That's great to hear. We missed you, but at least now you can both meet Chelsea and Finn."

Finn stood to greet them as Jack explained that the two cowboys, both wranglers at the Last Chance, had become a popular entertainment duo in the area. Trey Wheeler handled the vocals and the older man, who went only by Watkins, played backup.

"And you're here to play for us?" Chelsea looked like a kid on Christmas morning. "That's so generous of you!"

"We love to play, ma'am," Trey said with a winning smile. "When Jack called and said you'd like some dancing music, we were only too happy to oblige. Now if you'll excuse us, we'll go set up. We'll play a few background tunes while you eat, but when you're ready to dance, give us a signal."

Finn glanced at their host after the two men left. "I appreciate this, Jack. It's above and beyond."

"Glad to do it." His dark eyes flashed with amusement. "Can I have the first dance?"

13

THE DEBATE OVER whether Jack would be dancing with Finn continued as they ate dinner and enjoyed some mellow tunes provided by the two guitarists. Finn insisted that he'd learned enough and Jack maintained that he could use another lesson. Chelsea got a kick out of listening to them trade barbs.

Eventually the conversation turned to other topics, specifically Jack's new interest in Seattle. But when they'd all finished eating, Jack's attention swung back to dancing.

"You'll never have a better opportunity to polish your moves than right now with the place practically deserted, O'Roarke. In a little while word will get out that Trey and Watkins are playing and we'll have a crowd." He sounded quite reasonable except for the devilish gleam in his eyes.

Finn finished his beer. "Why do you care if my moves are polished or not?"

"Professional pride. If you go around telling people I taught you and you can't dance worth a lick, that will reflect poorly on me."

"That's the most ridiculous thing I've ever heard. And,

besides, I don't need any more lessons. I understand the basics."

"You know just enough to be dangerous, cowboy. I'm sure Chelsea would love for you to become more skilled." He looked to her for support.

"Hey, hey." She made a shooing motion. "Leave me out of this."

"Oh, all right." Finn tucked his napkin beside his plate. "Let's do this thing, Jack." As Trey and Watkins struck up a lively two-step, Finn and Jack took the floor.

"Finn's a good sport." Josie smiled as she watched them. "Jack loves trying to throw guys off balance by insisting on improving their dance skills. He admires the ones who go along with it."

"I think it's great. Finn has a tendency to take things too seriously. Jack's a good influence." She chuckled as Jack went into a twirl in one direction and Finn spun out in the other. Then Jack demonstrated the underarm twirl and hats flew.

Josie rolled her eyes. "Or a bad influence, depending on your perspective." She glanced over at Chelsea. "But Jack went through a serious phase, too."

"Really? It seems so much a part of his personality to joke around."

"It is, but he buried his sense of humor for a while. He had issues. I sense that Finn does, too."

"Yep."

"All you can do is love them and hope they figure it out."

"So true." Chelsea gave a short answer because she didn't want to call attention to that casual remark. At least, it seemed casual, and yet it contained a loaded word.

Chelsea had avoided *love* in connection with Finn.

She'd always preferred to think she was in lust with him. But today hadn't been about lust.

Instead it had been about walking hand-in-hand, sharing conversations and discovering facets of each other's personality. She'd seen a different side of him when they'd met Harley and Wilbur. Just now she'd learned that the same man who'd been captivated by a story about a pig saved by a noble little spider could also become completely immersed in the details of a new friend's cherished project.

It seemed as if getting sex out of the way meant that she could view him as a whole person without the static of constant frustration blurring the picture. She liked what she saw. And he was turning into one fine dancer, too.

When he and Jack came back to the table, they were both grinning.

"We're going to be on TV before you know it," Jack said. "O'Roarke can now officially shake his booty."

"All because of you, Jack. All because of you." Finn held out his hand to Chelsea. "May I have this dance, sweet lady?"

"You'd better believe it." She took his hand and walked with him out to the dance floor. The rubber tread on her shoes squeaked, reminding her that she didn't have on the right footwear. "Hang on a minute. I'll be right back."

She met Jack and Josie coming out to the floor. Jack lifted his eyebrows. "I hope you're not going to make that boy dance all by his lonesome."

"Nope. Just handling a slight problem." She sat and quickly took off both socks and shoes. Dancing in sock feet sounded like a recipe for slipping and falling. She'd dance barefoot.

When she returned, Finn looked at her bare toes and shook his head. "I don't trust myself."

"That's okay." She grabbed his hand and pulled him onto the floor. "I trust you completely."

He tugged her into his arms and looked into her eyes. "Foolish woman." But he was smiling, and as he spun her around, he didn't step on her once.

She discovered that she loved dancing barefoot. Josie and Jack were the only other ones on the floor, which gave both couples plenty of room. Jack became something of a showoff, executing complicated steps that involved lots of dips and twirls.

But Finn just…danced with her. Holding her gaze, he used only light pressure to communicate his moves and she wondered if she'd have needed even that. It was as if she could read his mind. They synchronized their footwork effortlessly and she was sorry when the music ended.

She sighed. "That was the best."

Happiness shone in his eyes. "It was. I was so worried I'd step on you, but then somehow I knew I wouldn't."

"We were in the zone."

He laughed. "We were."

"Nice job out there." Jack walked over and clapped Finn on the back. "I knew you had guts, O'Roarke. You wouldn't catch me wearing boots and dancing with a barefoot lady."

"I can't explain why, but I felt like I could do it with my eyes closed."

Jack regarded him silently. Then he gave a short nod. "You'll do." And he went back to Josie as the music started again with a slower tune.

"I haven't known him long," Chelsea said, "but I'm guessing that's high praise."

"Could be." Finn scooped her back into his arms and began an easy circuit around the floor. "But there's only one person in this room I want to impress, and I'm dancing with her."

"For the record, I'm impressed. It's been a terrific day."

He urged her closer and murmured in her ear. "But the sun's going down."

"Mmm-hmm."

"I'm ready for the day to end and the night to begin."

"Me, too." After two nights of making love to him, the desperate, unbearable hunger had been replaced with a steady hum of awareness. After today, tonight would be good. Very good.

Jack had been right that word would spread about the unexpected live entertainment. Customers drifted in, either because a friend had alerted them or they'd heard music spilling into the street. Eventually the once-empty dance floor became crowded.

The four of them agreed it was time to leave. Jack won the fight over the bill by calling it a tax deduction for Josie, and they walked outside together.

"It's been a pleasure." Jack shook hands with Finn and hugged Chelsea.

"That's an understatement." Josie hugged them both. "We'll be thinking of you this week."

"And if that last little bit doesn't show up," Jack said, "you know who to call."

"Thanks." Finn smiled. "We've got this."

"We do," Chelsea said. "And thank you for all you've done."

"Yes, thank you." Finn wrapped an arm around her shoulders.

As they said their last goodbyes, Chelsea stood in the warm circle of Finn's embrace with a cool evening breeze ruffling her hair. A week ago she'd been worried that

Thunder Mountain Academy might not happen. A week ago she'd wondered if her crush on Finn was doomed. Now anything was possible.

They rode back to the Bunk and Grub in cozy silence. Nothing needed to be said. They both knew what lay ahead and anticipation vibrated between them.

The lobby was the same as before, with low lamplight and the scent of cinnamon in the air. The scene was familiar yet completely different because she and Finn were different. They climbed the stairs without rushing, yet she felt his solid presence behind her, knew he was as focused on her as she was on him.

She unlocked her door without trembling, but her heart thumped wildly as she walked inside. She'd never made love with someone when her heart was so full. The housekeeper had left a light on and folded back the covers. The door clicked shut and she turned to face him.

Slowly he took off his hat and laid it on the dresser. Then he dragged in a breath and spoke for the first time since they'd left the saloon. "You're everything I've ever wanted, and I'm scared to death."

Her heart ached for him. That couldn't have been easy for him to admit. "I'm scared, too. I've never felt this way."

"Neither have I, and I'm convinced I'll mess it up."

She was fully aware that he might, but she wasn't going to let that keep her from loving him now. "We only get scared when we worry about the future. If we just think about what's happening right now, then we won't be afraid."

He squeezed his eyes shut. "Yeah. We went over that."

She couldn't help smiling. "It's not easy to remember. It should be, but it's not."

Opening his eyes, he moved toward her. "Right now

I'm in the bedroom of a beautiful woman who is going to let me make love to her."

"Right now I'm waiting for an outrageously sexy cowboy to kiss me."

He smiled. "Damn. Should've kept on the hat."

"No, it only gets in the way."

"Can't have that." Gathering her close, he covered her mouth with his.

And then everything was okay. There was no past, no future. Only this—his lips moving against hers, his tongue seeking, his breath warm, his hands gently exploring, caressing, arousing her until she molded her body against the steady heat that was Finn.

As they slowly undressed each other, she thought of the effortless way they'd danced. Sliding out of their clothes had the same fluid motion. No rush, no awkwardness. She'd never been so in tune with a lover.

The clothes lay in a glorious heap on the floor. She threw back the covers and he lifted her into his arms so he could lay her in the exact center of the bed. Then he stepped back and gazed at her.

"Finn?" She stretched out her hand toward him.

"I need to look. Let me."

"You've seen me this way before."

"I have. But…I know you better now."

Then she understood. She knew him better, too. She'd explored the many layers of Finn O'Roarke today, and he was more precious to her because of that. Even though they'd seen each other naked before, they'd never truly seen each other.

His intense blue gaze roamed over her, heating her in ways that even his touch did not. She squirmed against the sheets, wanting him to hold her, stroke her, love her. "Finn, please."

With a soft groan he came to her. He kissed her forehead, her eyelids, her cheeks and her mouth. "I can't wait," he murmured. "I need you now."

"Don't wait."

He pulled out the bedside table drawer where he'd stashed the condoms and wasted no time putting one on. Then he moved over her and held her gaze. "Right now I'm sinking deep inside you." And he joined them together with one firm thrust.

She gasped with pleasure. "Right now I'm feeling great joy."

"Is that right?" He pulled back and pushed home again. "This brings you joy?"

"Oh, Finn, you know it does." She wrapped her arms around his muscled back.

"I want to bring you joy."

Her smile trembled as she gazed up at him. "That's very nice to know."

"You deserve buckets of joy." He settled into a steady rhythm.

She focused on those amazing blue eyes. "So do you."

"Right now I'm finding it with you."

Her heart swelled. "Same here, cowboy."

"If only…" He paused to gulp in air. "If only we could stay like this forever."

"But we're here now."

"Yes." He slowed his pace. "We are." His gaze locked with hers. "I'm with you, Chels."

"I'm with you, Finn." They moved together as if they were dancing, his hips keeping perfect time with hers. And because they were so closely attuned, they knew when the energy shifted, when their bodies needed more.

He increased the pace and she responded with a whimper of need. Together they reached for shared glory and found it. She held on tight as they shuddered in each other's arms. Perfection. Was she crazy to want more?

THIS TIME FINN stayed and she woke to find him spooning her, her back tucked against his chest and his arms around her waist. She lay quietly and thought about what their future had in store. The Bunk and Grub had turned out to be a private hideaway, but tonight they'd be separated.

She wanted to visit Thunder Mountain Ranch, but if it meant severing this connection with Finn, that took some of the shine off the prospect. He'd promised they'd go on horseback rides into the boonies so they could have private time. She couldn't imagine how that could be as cozy as snuggling in this bed.

"I can hear you thinking." His breath was warm against the back of her neck.

"I'm getting used to sharing a bed with you."

"I know." He sighed. "I haven't prepared Rosie and Herb for that and I don't want to spring it on them."

"And you shouldn't. Don't mind me. We'll manage."

"But it won't be like this." His arms tightened around her and he nuzzled behind her ear.

"No." She surrendered to his sweet caresses, knowing that soon they'd have to sneak off to do this, and this, and, oh, yes, *this*. He gave her a climax first with his clever fingers and then he ripped open another condom so they could both enjoy the experience.

As they lay flopped on their backs, gasping and sated, she reached over and slipped her hand in his. "Whatever happens is fine," she murmured. "I don't want to be greedy."

"I do." He lifted her hand to his lips. "I'm spoiled rotten after this weekend. I'm not about to take a vow of celibacy."

"Then I'll follow your lead."

"We'll have private time. I promise you." He nibbled on her fingers and then began to suck on them. Before long they'd made use of another condom. It was as if they both realized that the game was about to change.

They left the Bunk and Grub later than planned, but that was mostly because he couldn't seem to stop making love to her. She wasn't about to object. Her room had become a haven where they could explore these new feelings and she was as loath to give it up as he was.

Breakfast was over by the time they headed downstairs, but Yvonne gave them a thermos of coffee and some pastries in a bag. Pam was there to check them out and hug them both goodbye. On the way out to the SUV, Chelsea reminded Finn that he'd been looking forward to the trip to Thunder Mountain Ranch, but that didn't seem to help either one of them. Reluctantly they loaded up and drove away.

Chelsea wasn't in the mood to work, either. But if she expected to have something for her new client's PR campaign by the time she arrived home, she should put in some hours on it now. Feeling less than inspired, she opened her laptop.

Finn glanced over at her. "How about a little music?"

"Sure, why not?"

He flipped on the radio and a country station came on. "Is that okay?"

"That's fine." But the country music reminded her of all the dancing they'd done this past weekend. Would that be the last time she'd get to dance with Finn?

"I feel as if I've been evicted from paradise."

She blew out a breath. "So do I, and that's crazy. We've been looking forward to visiting Thunder Mountain together. You said you wanted to show me all your old haunts."

"Which I do. That'll be fun."

"Plus I'll be able to meet everyone, finally, and see the birthplace of Thunder Mountain Academy. We can all celebrate, knowing the Kickstarter campaign is in the bag. Does it matter so much that we won't be able to sleep in the same bed at night?"

"Yes. Yes, it does."

"We've spent our whole lives not doing that. We've only shared a bed for three nights, and one of those wasn't even the whole night because you left. We should be able to handle this."

"I've been telling myself that ever since I woke up this morning, but the prospect of not having you close by is depressing the hell out of me."

"So what are we going to do?"

"I don't know yet. I'm working on it."

She decided not to point out the obvious, that they'd made no commitment to each other. Once they returned to Seattle, they'd be sleeping miles apart. Had he thought of that?

She had. Because they'd have to separate eventually, worrying about their current situation made no sense. But she must be as bonkers as Finn, because she didn't want to be apart from him, either.

14

WHILE CHELSEA WORKED on her laptop, Finn had plenty of time to think. He *really* didn't want to be apart from her every night they stayed at Thunder Mountain Ranch. When he considered his strong negative reaction to that potential separation he finally admitted that he was falling for her. Or, more likely, had fallen.

If so, he wouldn't magically get over her when they went back to Seattle. He'd want to be with her then, too. Maybe it wouldn't work out because he'd return to his usual anal mode, but maybe he'd changed.

By the time they stopped for lunch in Thermopolis, he'd decided what to do. But he had to run it past Chelsea first. Come to think of it, this conversation could turn out to be pretty damned important. Depending on how she reacted, he'd get a better sense of how she felt about him.

They ordered a couple of burgers and some fries at a cozy little diner that she'd found using TripAdvisor on her phone. The diner would have been right at home in Shoshone, or in Sheridan, for that matter. He was glad she was charmed by small Western towns and down-home eateries, but he wasn't surprised. Her enthusiasm for life in general had endeared her to him from the first day they'd met.

They sipped coffee while they waited for their food. Now that the moment was here, he had a slight case of nerves. He decided not to leap right into the heart of the matter. "How's the project coming along?"

"Good." She nodded. "I wasn't sure whether I'd be focused enough to get anything done, but I made some progress. I think he'll like what I've come up with."

"Why wouldn't you be focused?"

"Oh, you know. Wondering how things will work out at Thunder Mountain."

Perfect opening. "I have a solution for how to handle our sleeping arrangements, but before I call Rosie, I need your okay."

She blinked. "Call Rosie?"

"I don't like the thought of sneaking around to have sex."

"Neither do I, but I thought we had no choice."

He thumbed back his hat and sighed. "That's because I was thinking like a seventeen-year-old boy instead of a man. I'd like to call Rosie and explain that we're used to sleeping in the same room and we both think it would be fun to stay in the cabin. But there's no bathroom in it. The bathhouse is a short walk away. And it has four bunks, not one bed."

She grinned. "Sounds just like summer camp."

"I know it's a little primitive, but my plan is to push the mattresses together on the floor. I won't kid you, though. It won't be nearly as comfy as the guest bed in the house."

"But you'll be there, which more than makes up for the lack of an innerspring."

"Thank you, ma'am." He reached across the table and

took her hand. "So you'd be okay with me announcing that to Rosie?"

"There's a lot to like about your plan, but I thought you said Rosie was a matchmaker. Won't she expect us to have made some kind of commitment? We don't want to mislead her."

His chest tightened. "I don't plan to mislead her."

"So you'll explain that this is temporary? You said she might not like that, either."

"Look, I don't know where this thing with us will end up." He captured her hand between both of his. "But I don't want to stop seeing you when we get back to Seattle."

She went very still and her eyes widened. "You don't?"

"No." He took a shaky breath. "But I might still be the anal control freak I was when I left. I think I might be changing, learning, but it's hard to know when we're in a completely different environment."

"You want…" She swallowed. "You want to do a test run when we get back? Is that what you're suggesting?"

"Yes, ma'am." He stroked her palm with his thumb. "But if you're not willing to try that, I completely understand. You've seen me at my worst and if you—"

"I'm willing to try that." Her voice was breathy and her eyes still reflected shock. "I just never expected you to say this. What…how would we…?"

"I thought maybe…this is just an idea, now, but I thought that you'd let me stay with you for a little while. See how it goes. I'd keep my place just in case, but I'd pay my share of the food and help with utilities. And you could throw me out anytime you wanted to."

"Oh, Finn." She trembled. "It's a big step."

"You don't want to." His heart ached. "I don't blame you. It was just a possibility. We can forget I mentioned it. We could just date. I could live with that. I just don't want everything to go back to the way it was. I want to be with you. Dating would be better than nothing."

"It would be stupid. I don't want to date you. I want to be with you every night. That's what this whole thing with Rosie is about. I hate the thought of sleeping in the house while you're in the cabin."

"So…" He was confused. "What are you saying?"

"I'm saying that it's a big step, but if you're game, I'm game."

His stomach bottomed out. "Chels, are you sure?"

"I'm sure that I want to try. You're right that it might not work, but if we just assume that, then we have nothing. I'd rather try and go through hell if it doesn't work than miss out on a chance at heaven if it does."

"I feel like dragging you out of that chair and kissing you until your toes curl."

Fire flashed in her brown eyes. "Better not start something you can't finish."

He groaned. "I didn't figure this out very well. I need to call Rosie and we should eat. Then we have to make tracks if we're going to get there by dinnertime. That's when she's expecting us and I'm sure she'll cook something special."

"So we postpone our make-out session. Think about this. By calling Rosie, you're setting us up to spend the night together. Short-term sacrifice for long-term gain. You're a business owner. I'm sure you know all about that."

"I've never had to sacrifice kissing you."

She gazed at him. "Yes, you have. You've been sacrificing that for five years."

"Good point. That's why I have so much catching up to do."

"Go make your phone call. I'll be here when you get back."

"Okay." He squeezed her hand and released it. "If the order comes, start eating. Don't wait for me."

"Should we ask them to fix it to go? Then we could leave that much sooner."

He glanced at the time on his phone. "No, we should be fine. Let's stay and enjoy the meal." He smiled at her. "Be right back."

CHELSEA WATCHED HIM head through the door and then she was able to see him through the restaurant's front window as he paced back and forth while he made his call. He still had that cowboy saunter going on, and she noticed more than one woman take a second look as they passed by. *Too late, ladies! He just said he wants to move in with me.*

She still couldn't believe it. After years of frustration, she would get the chance she'd yearned for—to see if they could be a couple. And not just here, where he felt removed from the pressure cooker of his business. He was willing to risk putting it all on the line.

He hadn't mentioned love, but knowing Finn, he wouldn't toss that word into the mix until he thought they had a decent shot at making it together. No point in telling someone you love them and then having to swear off that person for the rest of your life. She felt the same way, although the emotion rolling through her had to be connected to that four-letter word. Either that or she was coming down with the flu.

Right after their food arrived, he came back in wearing a puzzled expression. She'd expected a smile. "Did you talk to her?"

"I did." He put his napkin in his lap. "And she made

me promise to relay the message that she's superexcited to meet you."

"Same here. But what about the cabin thing?" Her burger was huge, so she cut it in two before starting to eat. "How did she react to that?" She took a juicy bite.

"Knowing Rosie, I think she's messing with me. I explained the situation, which made her very happy that I'm involved with someone, especially someone she can get to know. She never met Alison." He picked up his entire burger, but then, he had the hands for it. "She and Herb had planned to fly up to see us but we were fighting all the time and I told them not to come." He took a healthy bite.

"I guess I'd better be on my best behavior, then."

He swallowed his bite. "Your behavior is always your best, even when you're being snarky."

"I'm going to start getting that way if you don't tell me what she said about the cabin. Are we sleeping together or not?"

"I'm pretty sure we are, but she said the Brotherhood cabin—that's what we call the one all three of us stayed in—wasn't a good idea and she had a better one."

"She's not giving us a guest room in the house, after all, is she?"

"I doubt it." He put down his burger and grabbed a fry. "I raved on about how much you would love staying in a real log cabin, that it would be a whole new experience for you."

"No, it won't."

"You've stayed in one before?"

"Sure, at summer camp. That's why I made that remark when you mentioned bunks and a bathhouse that's a short walk away."

"Oh. Well, I didn't know that." He looked a little disappointed as he went back to eating his burger.

She found that adorable. "But I've never stayed in a log cabin with you, so what you told her is true. It will be a whole new experience. And for the record, I loved summer camp, so walking outside to the bathhouse will bring back good memories."

"That's assuming we stay in one of the cabins. I'm not sure what Rosie's up to. All she said was that I'd be pleased."

"She sounds like a pip."

"None of us were a match for her. Herb's pretty easygoing and we could fool him sometimes with our shenanigans. Not Rosie. If she didn't call us on something we'd done, it was only because it was small potatoes and she didn't feel the need to deal with it."

Chelsea started on the second half of her burger. "You've called it the Brotherhood cabin twice now. Does each cabin have a name, like we did at camp?"

"No, just that one. Cade, Damon and I were the first three boys Rosie and Herb took in, and we called ourselves the Thunder Mountain Brotherhood. They started out using guest rooms for the boys, but eventually they built cabins. The three of us got the first one."

"Rank has its privileges."

"Oh, yeah, we lorded it over the others." He ate another fry. "We'd been through a blood brother ceremony and they hadn't, so we were special. It's a wonder any of them still speak to us."

"A ceremony? Really?"

"Actually, I wasn't invited. I was the third boy brought out to the ranch. Cade and Damon had been there for months and were buddies by then. They kind of ignored me."

"Aw."

"It's okay. I was odd man out. Kids are like that." He took another bite of his burger.

"I know, but you'd just lost your grandfather and now nobody wanted to be your friend."

He shrugged as if it hadn't mattered. She knew it had, but if he wanted to pretend otherwise, fine with her.

"To be fair," he said, "I was big on rules, which doesn't tend to make a kid popular."

"Anal, even then."

"Probably worse. Anyway, they snuck out of the house at midnight and I followed them. You weren't supposed to leave the house after lights-out. I hadn't decided whether to tell on them or not, but I scared the hell out of them walking up to their little campfire. When I realized what they were doing, I wanted in."

"And they let you."

"They probably didn't want to, but Cade gave me this look as if he knew it would hurt my feelings if they didn't. So I made a cut in my hand and pressed it against their cuts and we said a pledge Cade had written up. Thirteen-year-olds can be so melodramatic."

"I love this story. I'm so glad you told me before we got there." She hesitated. "Should I let on that I know?"

"Sure. It wasn't exactly a secret, like I said. Apparently Rosie knew we'd gone out there and listened to make certain we came back okay. We all wore bandages the next day, so I'm sure she figured out the whole thing."

"Do you remember where you had that little ceremony?"

"Absolutely. We all do." He munched on another fry, but he still hadn't finished his burger, as if he'd rather talk than eat. "We've joked about putting a plaque in the ground to commemorate it. I'd already planned to take you on a tour of the significant places on the ranch, and that's one of them."

"I'm so excited to go there now."

"Me, too, especially if the sleeping quarters turn out okay." He glanced at the time on his phone. "Speaking of that, we should head out."

"But you haven't finished your lunch."

"No worries. It's been fun telling you about that stuff. I'll get our waitress to box up the rest and I'll eat on the road while you get some more work done."

"Um, right."

"You're planning to work again, aren't you?" He caught the eye of the woman who'd been serving them.

"That was my original idea, but—"

"And it's a good one." He glanced up as the waitress came over. "Ma'am, we have to leave. I wonder if you could please box this up for me and bring the bill?"

"You've got it." She winked at him.

"Thank you, ma'am."

"Anytime." She smiled at him as she whisked away his plate.

He'd made another conquest but didn't seem to notice as he kept talking to Chelsea. "I have so much I want to show you when we get there, so the more you can do on the road, the better."

"True." Maybe she shouldn't admit how excited she was about his plan to move in with her. All through lunch the prospect had hovered in the back of her mind, demanding attention. She needed to think about practical things like making room in her closets and dresser drawers. Maybe she'd buy bath sheets because her towels weren't big enough for him.

But mostly she wanted to sit and contemplate the joy of taking a Sunday morning stroll to Pike Place Market for coffee and croissants, or cuddling on her sofa on a blustery winter's night watching TV—assuming they made it to winter, of course. They liked some of the same shows. She knew that from five years of animated conversation.

So much to think about and so much to anticipate. She doubted that she'd be able to concentrate on work now that he'd dropped his bombshell. But if she told him all that, she might spook him, and that was the last thing in the world she wanted to do.

"You're right," she said. "Using the rest of the trip to work on my client's project makes perfect sense."

"See, that's what I admire about you. You work when you need to work and you play when you want to play."

"Thank you." Okay, she'd definitely better work this afternoon if he was taking her as a role model. Now wouldn't be the time to stare out the car window daydreaming about the future.

"I've been paying attention to how you manage it. If I can learn to unplug instead of constantly thinking about work, you might not toss me out on my ass the first week."

"I won't toss you out the first week, no matter what. We should give ourselves time to adjust."

"You say that now, but you haven't lived with me when I'm in work mode. I made Alison miserable. I might make you miserable."

"No, you won't, because I understand what it's like to have responsibility for the entire operation. I'm not sure she did." She was determined not to rag on his ex, but drawing a few comparisons wouldn't hurt.

"I've thought about that. Her job was nothing like mine and she didn't get it. But I took the whole work thing to extremes, too."

"Sometimes you have to. I burned the midnight oil to

finish Saturday's presentation. If you'd been around then, you wouldn't have been able to get my attention." She wasn't positive about that but it sounded good. "When you're self-employed, sometimes you put in long hours and other times you give yourself time off."

"But I've never let myself take time off."

She smiled. "I know. We can work on that." And she had all kinds of ideas about how to coax him to relax and let go for a while. She could hardly wait to put them into practice. She'd been dreading the end of this trip and now...now it could be the beginning of something very wonderful.

15

BACK ON THE ROAD to Sheridan, Finn couldn't remember the last time he'd felt this happy. The weekend at the Bunk and Grub had been great and he'd cherish it forever, but he hadn't had a plan. He always felt better when he had one, and now he did. Or rather, they did.

Chelsea had agreed to give him a shot, and he couldn't ask for more than that. She probably had more faith in him than he had in himself. He was counting on that because his confidence sometimes got a little shaky when it came to a major overhaul of his normal routine.

But she seemed ready and willing to take on the challenge of rehabilitating a confirmed workaholic. From the corner of his eye he could see her typing on her laptop. The soft click of the keys soothed him, letting him know that she was in control of her habits in a way that he wasn't.

He could be, though, given the right motivation. If the promise of being with Chelsea wasn't enough motivation, then he was a hopeless case. He'd dreamed of it for five long years without ever thinking he could be that fortunate. Now a life with her was within his grasp.

Her little apartment wasn't huge, at least what he remembered of it. He'd only been there a couple of times because everything about the place had tempted him to stay. Her furniture had beckoned him to relax into the plump cushions, and the art she'd chosen was so Chelsea—abstract and cheerful.

As he recalled, the apartment had been tidy without being fussy. He had his hang-ups, but extreme neatness wasn't one of them. Living in chaos didn't appeal to him, but he could tolerate a little clutter, even liked it. Chelsea's place had struck that happy medium.

He wondered if her landlord allowed pets. She didn't have any, but that didn't mean there was a restriction. His apartment complex permitted certain pets in exchange for a hefty deposit. Not a pig, of course, but dogs, cats, fish and birds were fine. He'd checked that out before renting.

Then he'd made no move to adopt because his schedule was so insane. Back in June, Lexi had suggested he get two cats because they could keep each other company. But he'd never followed through. He still believed his lifestyle had to change first.

Maybe it was about to. And good thing he hadn't adopted a couple of cats. Asking if he could move in with Chelsea was one thing. Bringing along a couple of cats would be a lot more complicated.

As they drew closer to Sheridan, the landscape began to look familiar. He'd flown in from Seattle in June, but seeing it from the road was better. As he drove, the silhouette of the Big Horn Mountains shifted with the changing angle. Gradually the mountains assumed the burly shape that meant he was almost home.

No, not home, not really. He'd told Chelsea that he'd shifted his allegiance to Seattle and it was true. But these mountains would always tug at his heart.

Unlike the Grand Tetons of Jackson Hole, which thrust

skyward in dramatic jagged splendor, the Big Horns were more solid and broad shouldered. He appreciated the beauty of the Tetons and sitting on the porch at the Last Chance had given him a spectacular view of them. But these mountains calmed him in a way that the edgy Tetons never would.

"It's beautiful, isn't it?" Chelsea turned off her laptop and closed the cover. "So different from where we've just been, yet majestic."

"I love these mountains. Sometimes when I was afraid that my grandfather wouldn't be able to take care of me, I imagined that the mountains would." He felt her watching him. "When I was five or six. Not when I was older."

"Why not? It's a lovely thought and they do give you that feeling. They're muscular, in a way."

"That's a good way to describe them, but I don't want you to think I lived in some fantasy world."

"I know you didn't, but there's nothing wrong with a little fantasy now and then if it helps you cope with your problems. I'm glad you had these mountains. I can see why they'd be comforting."

Another knot loosened in his chest. He hadn't realized that he needed her to understand his connection to the mountains, but of course he did. He needed her to understand…everything. "I'm so glad you're here." He glanced over at her. "I should have had sense enough to bring you before without being roped into it."

"Doesn't matter." Her smile was warm. "I'm here now, and I can't wait for you to show me your old stomping grounds."

That made him think of something else. She probably needed him to understand everything about her, too. "We should go to Bellingham when we get back."

Her response was slow in coming. "Yes, I guess we should."

"You sound a little hesitant."

"Maybe because I keep thinking I'm going to wake up and find this was all a dream."

He took a deep breath. "Me, too. But I want it to be real, and that's why we should go to Bellingham. I've known you for five years, but I want to really *know* you. I want to meet your folks. I want to see where you went to school and where you hung out with your friends. You must have gone to the beach a lot."

"We did."

"I want to see what that beach looks like."

She reached over and squeezed his arm. "Thank you. Maybe this is real, after all."

"I'm determined to make it that way." He turned down the familiar road leading to Thunder Mountain Ranch. "We'll be there in about ten minutes. I just wish I knew what sort of arrangement Rosie has come up with."

"She said you'd be pleased."

"Yeah, but whatever it is, she'll milk it for all it's worth. Rosie likes to have her fun. From what I hear, she let Damon think he was going to work on the new cabin project over Fourth of July weekend with a guy named Phil. Turned out to be Philomena. You'll meet her at dinner tonight. They're together, now, which makes Rosie very happy."

"You weren't kidding about her matchmaking, were you?"

"No, ma'am."

"Lexi told me in an email that he was with someone and that he'd moved back to Sheridan, but she didn't mention the Phil-slash-Philomena twist. Why did Rosie let him think she was a guy?"

"Apparently, Damon had some old-fashioned ideas about women in male-oriented jobs and she wanted to give him a wake-up call."

"I see." Chelsea smiled. "I'm getting a better picture of Rosie with every new story. Anything else you should tell me about her?"

"When she was in the hospital last June, she gave everyone strict orders not to bring her flowers as if we thought she was about to croak. So Damon and Cade bought her a case of Bailey's. Needless to say there's still a lot of it left, so if you're a fan, then—"

"I am! I love Bailey's. A little bit in a cup of coffee in the evening is perfect."

"Then you two can bond over that. Nobody else likes the stuff, but it's her favorite." He looked forward to bringing Rosie and Chelsea together. He had a feeling they'd speak the same language. But he wished to hell Rosie had told him her plan. He wasn't big on surprises.

The road was a winding one, and he knew each curve by heart. A few more and he'd reach the turnoff to the ranch.

"We have to take a short dirt road to get there," he said, "but unlike Jack's washboard, this one will be graded."

"I'll admit that's the first time I've heard of someone deliberately keeping a road nearly impassable."

"I guess I understand it. It's such a landmark in the area that they could have tourists driving out for the hell of it. Rosie and Herb don't have to worry about that. Their place isn't anything like the Last Chance. It's a single-story ranch house."

"How big?"

"I'm not sure about the exact square footage, but it's larger than it looks from the front. They have five bedrooms. When they bought it they expected to have kids of their own. That didn't happen."

"I really admire their solution."

"I'm really grateful for their solution. The ranch is perfect for how they used it, especially once they added the cabins. You won't be able to see them when we drive in, but you'll see the barn and a corral off to the left. The front porch is nice, but it's not positioned to give you a mountain view like the one at the Last Chance."

"Not many places are like the Last Chance. So what kind of special meal do you think she's fixed to welcome you home?"

"I have a pretty good idea. All of us loved it when we lived here. When I tell you, you'll probably laugh."

"Lay it on me."

"Tuna casserole." He looked to see her reaction.

She didn't laugh, but she smiled. "With green peas in it and potato chips on top?"

"Yep." He could already taste it. "Nobody makes it like Rosie. I've tried, but it's never the same. I always ask for it when I visit, but I forgot this time because I wasn't coming straight here."

"I haven't had tuna casserole in years. My mom used to make it when I was a kid, but then she took a cooking class and got into fancy things with exotic ingredients. Tuna casserole disappeared from the menu."

"Too bad."

"I know! I hope Rosie makes it because now I want some."

"If she didn't, there's always tomorrow night. I guarantee she's got the fixings. Okay, here's the turnoff. Wow, somebody's put up a new sign." He pulled onto the dirt road and stopped so they could look at it.

"Very nice."

"No kidding."

Thunder Mountain Ranch was spelled out in elegant brass letters on a slab of polished wood positioned between two sturdy posts. From the bottom hung a second sign. Home of Thunder Mountain Academy was painted in the academy's colors of green and brown.

"I'll bet Damon made the hanging part after I called on Saturday. That would be like him."

"Or he and Phil did it together. You said she worked with him on the cabin."

"Could be. Whoever made it, it's beautiful."

"Let's remember to mention it when we get there. They might have worked hard to finish and hang it before we arrived."

"I'll bet they did." He glanced at Chelsea. "I've always known how much this means, but that sign…"

"It's very special," she said softly. "Now let's go meet your family and eat tuna casserole."

He smiled at her. "I like that you said *my family*."

"Well, they are, right?"

"They absolutely are." He started down the dirt road and was gratified at how smooth it was. Cade had probably been out here with the tractor recently. They rounded the bend and there stood the house. The eaves had recently been repainted and so had the Adirondack chairs on the front porch. Now the chairs alternated between Academy brown and Academy green.

"I love it, Finn," Chelsea murmured.

"Good. I was hoping you would." As he pulled into the gravel circular drive, one of the few similarities to the Last Chance Ranch, the front door opened and they all came out—Rosie, Herb, Cade, Lexi, Damon and a redhead who must be Philomena. His family. Heart full, he climbed out of the SUV and hurried around to open Chelsea's door.

But she was already out and moving toward the group spilling down the porch steps. "That sign is awesome!"

"I know!" Rosie held out her arms and gathered her in for a hug.

Finn stood transfixed by the sight, because it seemed so natural, as if Chelsea had been here dozens of times before.

Then Cade and Damon swarmed him, punching him on the arm and slapping him on the shoulder.

"I remember this hat!" Cade grabbed Finn's and switched with him, his gray eyes filled with laughter. "I wanted it but you saw it first."

"Yeah, and it looks a lot better on O'Roarke." Damon wore a battered straw cowboy hat over his sun-bleached hair. It would take a while for his surfer-dude image to fade after he'd spent four years in California. He glanced at Cade wearing Finn's hat. "Doesn't look broken in yet. You been hiding it in the closet, O'Roarke?"

"Pretty much."

"See there?" Cade settled it more firmly on his head. "He doesn't deserve such a fine hat. Hats get lonesome if they're not worn."

Finn laughed. "Then keep it, loser. I'm going to see my best girl." He spotted Rosie heading in his direction with a big grin on her face and love shining in her blue eyes.

Chelsea was now talking to Lexi and Phil, so Rosie must have made sure those three were hooked up before coming to see him. How like her. He pulled her into a bear hug that lifted her off her feet. "I love you, Mom."

"Same here, you big galoot. Now put me down. You're messing with my new outfit."

He set her down and surveyed the red jeans and sparkly top. "Nice job." Her blond hair had recently been styled and her red nails had some kind of glitter on them. But the main thing he noticed was that she looked healthy. Thank God.

"She bought her new duds three weeks ago after we found out you were coming." Herb moved in for his hug. "Good to see you, son."

"Good to see you, too, Dad." Finn could tell the guy had put on some much-needed weight. He'd always been wiry, but when Rosie was sick, he'd worried off some pounds he couldn't afford to lose. Now he felt solid again.

Herb stepped back and glanced over at Rosie. "You were right about the red. It looks good."

"It does, doesn't it? Never had red jeans before, but I decided Finn's arrival warranted something flashy."

"I'm honored."

"You should be." Rosie straightened the hem of her top. "And by the way, she's great." She angled her head toward Chelsea, who was carrying on an animated conversation with Lexi and Phil.

The three women made an interesting group with Lexi's short brown hair that tended to curl and Phil's red hair that reminded him of Lily's. Then of course there was his innovative Chelsea, who was forever adding interesting streaks of color to hers as if not satisfied to be plain blond. He watched as Damon and Cade walked over to be introduced. Chelsea gave each of them a big smile and shook hands. Lexi said something he couldn't hear and they all laughed.

Finn turned back to Rosie. "I'm glad you like her, but that was a really fast evaluation."

"Easy, though. After only a few minutes she's already comfortable here. She didn't wait for you to introduce her to me. She came right over on her own. And she's a good hugger. Not tentative or shy about it."

"She hugged me, too," Herb said. "She told us both that she admired our work with the foster program. That was nice to hear."

Finn glanced at Chelsea, who was listening intently to something Phil was saying. "She was eager to meet you."

"I was eager to meet her," Rosie said. "I went on her website and she normally charges a bundle for her services, but she's not charging us a dime. Of course, I know that's partly because she's in love with you, but still, she's being very generous."

In love? The simple statement caught him off guard. He supposed it was true, just as he supposed he was in love with her, but they hadn't said it to each other.

It wasn't an oversight on his part and he didn't think it was on hers, either. She'd probably come to the same conclusion he had. Using the *L* word should be saved until they'd made it through their trial run of living together. Any sooner than that would be asking for more heartache.

Rosie peered at him. "Are you feeling okay? You suddenly went sort of pale. I know you're paler than you used to be, but this was on top of your usual paleness. Come on inside and I'll get you some water. You're probably dehydrated." She turned toward the house.

"I'm fine, Mom. Don't worry about getting me any water. But I would like to know where you decided to put Chelsea and me tonight."

She turned back to him with a gleam in her eye. "Before we talk about that, you really need to meet Phil. She's been looking forward to you two getting here."

"Well, sure. That would be great." He tamped down his impatience.

"Come on over." She started toward the group gathered by the front steps. "Phil, you haven't had a chance to meet my boy Finn yet. Finn, this is Philomena Turner."

Phil had an open smile and a friendly blue gaze. She held out her hand. "It's good to finally meet you, Finn! Damon talks about you all the time."

"That must get annoying." Returning her smile, Finn shook hands with her. She had a firm grip, but then, this was a woman who could operate power tools, so no surprise there.

"Not annoying," Damon said. "Entertaining. She especially likes the one where you glued all the toilet seats shut and forgot that you had to use them, too. That gets a laugh every time, particularly the part where—"

"Yes, yes." Rosie rolled her eyes. "We've all heard that story a hundred times."

"I haven't." Chelsea smirked at Finn. "At least not all the way through."

"Well, Finn can tell you later." Rosie slipped an arm around her waist. "Right now let's take a walk so you and Finn can see the new cabin and the foundation for the rec hall."

Good thing Chelsea had worn her running shoes and not her sandals, Finn thought. "You're building a rec hall?" He glanced at Damon. "I haven't heard about that."

"We need one," Damon said as he fell into step beside Finn. "It'll be a combination dining hall, classroom and rec center. We decided the rec room in the house is too small for that many older teens, plus we don't need to have them bothering Rosie and Herb. They're students, not foster kids."

"I get that," Finn said, "but they'll need to be supervised out there."

"That's where I come in. Me and my new hat." Cade tipped it in Finn's direction. "I'll ride herd on 'em."

"Are you putting in a kitchen?" Finn hoped they weren't expecting to ferry food from the house.

Damon nodded. "Yep. You can add your two cents' worth on the choice of appliances if you want."

"I might just do that." He liked the idea of being involved in the nuts and bolts of the operation, and he had some expertise after supervising the remodeling of the space for O'Roarke's Brewhouse. "So did you make the academy sign this weekend?"

Damon grinned. "Like it?"

"I love it."

"Phil thought we should put one up after Rosie relayed your message on Saturday. We got Ben, our saddle maker guy, to help with the lettering. We didn't finish it until around noon. The paint's barely dry."

"Well, it's gorgeous."

"I helped hang it," Cade said.

"What he means is that he stood there and strawbossed the operation while Phil and I worked our asses off."

Finn nodded. "Yep, I can picture that."

"I knew my supervisory talents weren't properly appreciated." Cade sighed. "Without my discerning eye, that sign would've ended up all cattywampus."

"You were lucky it didn't end up around your neck." Damon made a grab for the hat.

"Hey! Hands off! Get your own." Cade settled it more firmly on his head. "Maybe O'Roarke's got another one tucked away in his closet, gathering dust."

"Nope. That's the only one I kept."

Damon gazed at him. "Not into the cowboy thing anymore?"

"I wasn't, but lately…" Without thinking, he looked over at Chelsea walking with Rosie.

Damon obviously noticed because he chuckled. "I see how it is. Nothing like boots and a hat, right, bro?"

"Let's say this. It doesn't hurt."

They reached the meadow where two months ago only three log cabins had stood. Now there were four, which created a semicircle around the large fire pit where he'd spent so many evenings roasting marshmallows and singing camp songs. The bathhouse looked the same, stretched out behind the group of cabins. Over to the right a foundation had been laid for the rec hall.

"Which one's the Brotherhood cabin?" Chelsea looked around the semicircle.

"The first one." Rosie pointed.

"You'll probably want to take a look at it," Phil said.

"Oh, definitely."

"But first let's show you the new one. Damon and I are really proud of it."

"That's fine. I want to see the results of your hard work. It looks great from the outside."

"Sure." Finn would show Chelsea the Brotherhood cabin later. He had a feeling they wouldn't be sleeping in it, though, which was disappointing. "You did a great job of matching it to the others."

"The main thing we changed was the foundation," Damon said as they all walked past the fire pit on their way to the cabin. "It's cement instead of block."

"You mean the floor won't squeak?" Finn couldn't imagine it.

"'Fraid not."

"I told him that went against tradition," Cade said. "If the floor doesn't squeak, how can you play music on it?"

"My point exactly. I got really good at 'Jingle Bells.'"

Damon looked pained. "Oh, for God's sake. A cement

foundation's sturdier. From a construction standpoint it makes sense."

"From a musical standpoint it sucks," Cade said. "But I didn't get a vote. Finn would've voted with me, too."

"I would have."

"Can't please everyone." Phil climbed up two cement steps and opened the cabin door. "We've all seen it, so why don't you two go in and look around?"

"Okay." Chelsea stepped inside and gasped. "Oh, my God."

Finn hurried in after her, afraid she'd found a giant spider or a snake. Instead she stood staring at a queen-size bed made up with sheets, a comforter and extra pillows. There were no bunks, but a couple of end tables had been placed on either side of the bed along with lamps. He whirled around and found Rosie leaning in the doorway.

She looked incredibly smug. "Will this do?"

16

CHELSEA WAS IN LOVE with these people. Rosie had welcomed her with open arms, literally, and because of Finn's earnest request, they would sleep in a real bed inside a brand-new log cabin. Over a celebratory dinner of tuna casserole in the cozy kitchen, Phil explained that they had discussed different configurations for the bunks and desks but hadn't decided yet how they wanted to build them.

"Phil had a great idea," Damon said. "She thinks if we create four loft beds in there with desks and a dresser underneath each one, it'll give each student his or her own territory. Now that the academy's a go, I'm in favor of retrofitting all the cabins that way."

Chelsea remembered her own teen years. "I would have loved it at that age." She glanced over at Rosie. "And in case I forget to say so, this is the best tuna casserole I've ever had in my life. But if you should meet my mother, you can't tell her I said so."

Rosie smiled. "Wouldn't dream of it."

"I believe I'll have some more." Finn picked up a casserole dish, one of two on the table, and began spooning more onto his plate.

"Yeah, me, too." Cade held out his empty plate. "Appreciate it. And a little extra for Ringo." He'd brought his gray tabby up to the house and Ringo was curled in a cat bed in the corner. A scoop of tuna casserole plopped in his food dish brought him running.

"Leave some for me." Damon grabbed the casserole when they were through. "Anybody else? I don't want to be a pig."

"Too late. I believe this is your fourth helping." Cade got up from the table. "Anyone need another one of the beers Finn so generously shipped over?"

"It's great beer," Herb said. "I'll have another one. Besides, we need to drink a few more toasts to the academy."

Chelsea also loved how they all raved about Finn's beer. It was good, but to hear them talk, no beer in the history of brewing had ever been so fine. Their loyalty warmed her heart.

"Speaking of pigs," Finn said, "I met a couple of awesome ones in Shoshone. It got me to thinking."

"No, Finn." Rosie met his gaze over the table. "No pigs. We had this discussion years ago. I love you to death and you brew a great beer, but we don't need pigs at Thunder Mountain."

"You should see his pictures, though," Chelsea found herself saying. "These are amazing pigs. One is named Harley and the other is named Wilbur."

"Wilbur's the name of the pig in *Charlotte's Web*!" Phil sat straighter. "I adored that book. I want to see your pictures, Finn."

The debate about pigs lasted for the rest of the meal with people choosing sides. Chelsea, Finn, Cade and Phil were pro-pig and Lexi, Damon, Rosie and Herb were antipig, at least as far as keeping one on the ranch. Despite Rosie's initial reaction, though, Chelsea thought she could be swayed.

After dinner and a quick cleanup, everyone decided to sit in the newly painted Adirondack chairs on the front porch. Most everyone had another beer, but Chelsea asked Rosie for some coffee laced with Bailey's. Rosie was delighted, and once she'd fixed their drinks, she chose a seat next to Chelsea.

Chelsea sipped her concoction and sighed. "Perfect. And thank you for setting us up in that cabin. It's awesome."

"All I did was come up with the idea. Damon and Cade dismantled one of our guest beds and hauled it down there along with a couple of nightstands and lamps. Lexi and Phil made up the bed. It was a group effort."

"Well, thanks to everyone, then. I can't imagine anything more special."

"You'll still have to trek to the bathhouse. That part couldn't be magically changed."

"I don't mind." She decided not to mention summer camp. Finn had told Rosie that this would be a brand-new experience. Better to keep quiet.

"I can't tell you how happy I am that he's found someone who understands him. He can be a bit of a control freak and a workaholic. I probably don't have to tell you that."

"No, but he's committed to learning when to let go. I'm hopeful he can."

"He can do all kinds of things when he's motivated. And he loves you so much."

She covered her gasp of surprise by taking another sip of her coffee. "Did he say that?"

"Not in so many words, but it's obvious. I know that boy, and I've never seen him look at a woman the way he looks at you. I don't know how he looked at his ex, of course, but he told us not to visit because they were fighting all the time, so it couldn't have been a good match."

"I don't think it was." Rosie's comment continued to swirl in her mind. *He loves you so much.* It gave her the courage to broach another topic. "By the way, I was there when Finn took the pig pictures."

"And I admit they were cute, but we don't need pigs around here."

"Did you know that *Charlotte's Web* was a lifeline for him when he was a kid, before he came here?"

"It was? I knew he had the book on his shelf, but I didn't think much about it. Lots of kids like that book."

"I'm no psychologist, but I think that story of courage and sacrifice helped keep him going when he lived with his grandfather."

"Huh." Rosie took another drink of her coffee. "I didn't realize that. If I had, I might have listened more closely when he asked for a pig."

"He's still asking."

"But he doesn't live here anymore." Rosie glanced at her. "What's the point?"

"He'd see the pig when he visited, and if he successfully changes his attitude, he'll visit more often."

Rosie laughed. "So he can see the pig?"

"*No.* To see all of you, of course. The pig would be a bonus. The thing is, I found out this weekend that lots of potbellied pigs are abandoned once they become adults, so there's a need for people who have some acreage to take them in."

Rosie lifted her coffee mug in tribute. "Chelsea, darlin', I can tell you're in PR. You know exactly what to say to get my attention."

"To be honest, this is more for Finn than the pigs.

When I saw him with Harley and Wilbur, it touched my heart."

"So you're saying that if I adopt one of these abandoned pigs, it'll be good for the pig and good for someone I love?"

"That's what I'm saying. And the students would learn something by having that pig around, too. They can spread the word that cute little potbellied pigs get big and need plenty of room and that they're intelligent and trainable, like dogs."

"You are a persuasive young woman, Chelsea Trask." She stood. "More coffee and Bailey's? I'm having another."

"Then I will, too. Thank you, Rosie."

When Rosie went in to refill their mugs, Finn left his chair on the other side of the porch and came over to crouch in front of hers. "How soon can we excuse ourselves?"

"Not real soon. Rosie's getting us a refill and I think I just convinced her to adopt a pig."

He grinned. "You're kidding."

"Would I kid about a thing like that?"

The light on the porch was dim, but it was enough to gauge the flash of emotion in his eyes. "No, you wouldn't." He gave her knee a little squeeze. "When you think we can go, give me a signal."

"I will. And, Finn, I love your family."

He smiled. "So do I."

He loves you so much. She had to believe it was true. He was capable of loving deeply. He felt that way about everyone else on this porch with the exception of Phil, but he'd only just met her. He'd known the rest of them for fifteen years, and he cherished them all. She heard it in his voice, even when he was joking around. Especially then.

Rosie came back and handed Chelsea a mug. "I knew eventually I'd find someone else who likes Bailey's as much as I do. You'll have to visit a lot so you can help me make a dent in that case of it they bought me when I was in the hospital."

"Sounds good." Chelsea cradled the warm mug in both hands. "Finn's business anchors him in Seattle, but I can tell he's left a part of himself here. He needs to come back often and connect with his family."

"I think so, too. I've tried not to be one of those mothers who guilts their children into coming back to visit. That's obnoxious. But in the case of these foster boys, they do need to come back. It may be more important than if I'd given birth to them."

"I agree." She lifted her mug. "Let's drink to that."

That started a whole new string of toasts. She and Rosie lifted their mugs to several things, including the joys of tuna casserole, the appeal of a man in a Stetson and imaginative hair color. Rosie decided that her next salon visit might include lavender.

From there they moved on to movies and TV, where they matched up almost exactly. They turned thumbs down on slasher films and toasted action-adventure flicks with a touch of romance and a gorgeous hero. Rosie reluctantly admitted to following celebrity gossip and Chelsea confessed to having a stash of gossip magazines in her apartment.

When they'd both finished their second mug of coffee, Rosie gazed at her. "I've loved every minute of this, but you need to collect your sweetie pie and head on down to the cabin. We get up early around here."

"How early?"

"I serve breakfast at five-thirty."

Chelsea blinked. "All righty, then." She stood. "I'll just carry this into the kitchen and we'll be on our way."

"Never mind. I'll take your mug." She raised her voice. "Finn, honey, it's time to saddle up your SUV and drive Chelsea over to the cabin."

He was on his feet immediately and a round of hugs followed. It was almost like a bride and groom leaving the reception for the honeymoon, minus the wedding ceremony. Chelsea felt as if they were being given everyone's blessing.

As they took a back road around to the cabins, Chelsea glanced at Finn, who was still wearing Cade's brown Stetson. "Your brothers won't pull any pranks on us tonight, will they?"

He grinned. "Worried?"

"After being around them for a few hours…yeah. And I just realized there are no curtains on any of those windows."

"They won't pull anything. We mostly only do stuff to each other. When a guy's with his girl, he's off-limits unless he's being really obnoxious. Or she is. Damon and Cade think you're terrific, and they're so grateful for your help with this project. They wouldn't do anything that might scare you off."

"I'm the opposite of scared off. I'll probably bug you to come back a lot."

"Works for me. Do you really think Rosie will adopt a pig?"

"I do, but I'd let the subject lie. She obviously likes creating a ta-da moment."

He laughed. "You have her pegged."

"So here's my thought. Don't mention it again, and chances are a pig will be here the next time you visit."

"You could be right."

"Someone will need to contact Lily to set up her guest lectures, so it'll all fall neatly into place."

"Mostly because you backed me up and made that pitch to Rosie after dinner. That kind of support means a lot to me."

"I'm glad." Oh, yeah, he loved her and she loved him right back. They just weren't saying the word. "I wouldn't have thought to do it, though, if you hadn't told me about the book. I'm honored that you trusted me enough to explain how special it is to you."

"It is." He paused. "And so are you."

"Back atcha, cowboy." And that might be as close as they'd come to declaring their love, at least until they'd weathered a few weeks together in Seattle.

She was fine with that. She knew how much he cared for her just by listening to his voice. It had the same richness as when he spoke about his family. Rosie could hear it, too, no doubt. Probably everyone could because they knew him so well.

He parked next to the cabin. Aided by the moon and lamplight shining through the windows, they made their way to the cabin door. Someone must have turned on the lamps earlier.

Finn put himself in charge of both suitcases again and she carried the laptops. She breathed in pine-scented air and the aroma of fresh-cut wood. Heavenly.

She leaned the laptop cases in a corner. The bed and nightstands had been positioned against the back wall, which had no window, and a couple of braided rugs had been placed on either side of the bed. Otherwise the room was empty.

But full of love. She met Finn's gaze. "It's so beautiful."

"No, it's just nice. You're beautiful." He set his hat on top of his suitcase before walking toward her and pulling her gently into his arms. "Inside and out."

"Pretty words." She wound her arms around his neck. "Can I steal them?"

"You can have anything of mine you want."

"How about all of you?" Gazing into his warm blue eyes, she began unsnapping his shirt.

"I'm all yours." He dropped a soft kiss on her mouth. "But first let's turn out the lights." He released her and walked over to one of the nightstands.

"I thought you weren't worried about being disturbed?" She nudged off her running shoes.

"I'm not. I just prefer moonlight." He rounded the bed and turned off the other lamp. Sure enough, the nearly full moon cast a swath of silvery light over the bed.

"Impressive. Did you know that would happen?"

"I guessed it would. I wanted to see if I was right." He drew back the covers to reveal snowy sheets, and she heard the thumps of his boots as they hit the floor.

"I've never made love in the moonlight." Their breathing was the only sound in their darkened, private world. She shivered in anticipation.

"You're going to love it." His bare feet whispering across the wooden floor, he closed the distance between them and pulled her into his arms with the assurance of a man who knew he was wanted.

And, oh, how she wanted him. But the frenzy of those first nights had given way to an urge to tantalize and caress, to savor and explore. They undressed each other more deliberately tonight, each of them taking time to place kisses on the bare skin they uncovered.

Her sense of touch grew sharper in the deep shadows surrounding the bed. The merest brush of his fingertips sent heat spiraling through her veins. The moist pressure of his mouth tightened the coil of desire until she ached for him.

When all their clothes lay discarded on the floor, he swept her up in his arms and carried her to the bed. He laid her gently on the soft sheets and moved aside so his shadow didn't fall on her.

"Look at you," he murmured. "Glowing in the moonlight like a goddess. I could almost convince myself you're not real."

She held out her hand. "Come here and I'll convince you I'm very real."

"And if I touch you, you won't disappear? Or turn me to stone?"

"The only way you'll get in trouble, buster, is by *not* touching me. And I'll bet a part of you has already turned to stone."

Laughing, he climbed into bed with her. "You have a smart mouth, you know that?"

"So I've been told."

He moved over her. "So I guess you're not a goddess."

"Not last time I checked." She wrapped her arms around the solid warmth of his back as he propped himself up on his forearms. "But I think you must be a wizard."

"Why's that?" Bracing himself on one arm, he began a leisurely caress, stroking her throat, her shoulder and the curve of her breast.

He left a trail of sparks in his wake and she smoldered under the light pressure of his palm. "You must be a wizard." She took an unsteady breath. "Because you can turn a rational, intelligent woman into a lusty wench who would do anything—*anything*—to have you between her thighs."

"Good to know." He settled himself there, his rigid cock pressed against her belly. "My boots are dusty from this trip. They sure could use polishing."

"Almost anything. I draw the line at polishing your boots." She was bluffing. When she could feel the hard length of him *right there*, she'd agree to any terms he cared to set.

"Looks like I'm not a wizard, after all."

"Yes, you are." She reached between them. "Look, I found your staff." And holding all that leashed power sent moisture to the very spot where that staff needed to be.

He sucked in air. "Careful. It's hard to control a wizard's staff unless you know the magic word."

"Condom?"

"That would be it." He reached toward the nightstand. "And, presto! One magically appears."

"You can't fool me. You had it there all along."

"Nope. Plucked it out of thin air. That's what wizards do." He brushed it over her nose. "Care to put it on for me, lusty wench?"

"I suppose." She could barely breathe, she wanted him so desperately. She put the condom on him with trembling fingers.

His breathing roughened. "Well done, wench." Lifting his hips, he probed her gently before sliding partway in. "Now how about those boots?"

She gripped his firm buns. "Consider them polished."

"Excellent." He thrust home. Then he held very still as he gazed down at her. "I've been such a fool. Thank God I woke up."

"So I don't have to polish your boots?"

"Just be there for me, Chels." He began a slow, steady rhythm. "That's all I need."

"That's all I need, too." She held on tight as he rocketed them both skyward. She'd warned him to stay in the present. She needed to take her own advice.

17

LIFE DOESN'T GET any better than this. Finn had heard people toss out that statement dozens of times over the years. In his opinion, it had showed a lack of imagination. Life could always get better, right?

Well, no. Nothing could improve on the joy he felt sharing these few days and nights with Chelsea on the beloved ranch he'd called home for ten years, surrounded by the people he considered family. Both Cade and Damon were staying in town with their respective girlfriends, but they spent most of their time at the ranch working on academy projects.

Finn and Chelsea helped wherever they could, but this morning they'd taken a break to ride along the Forest Service Road. Rosie had suggested saddling up Navarre and Isabeau, a chestnut gelding and dark gray mare. Both were beautifully trained and Chelsea turned out to be a fair rider. They even cantered a little.

Then, in a secluded meadow with only the birds and forest creatures around, they'd made sweet love on a blanket in the sunshine. She'd insisted that he had to wear his Stetson to keep the sun out of her eyes. He thought she was just enamored of the hat.

She confirmed that as they returned to the barn and began unsaddling the horses. "I liked the gray hat, but Cade's right. His brown one is broken in. It looks more authentic and cowboy-ish. You're taking it back to Seattle, I hope."

"I am. Although I'm not sure why." He pulled off the saddle and carried it into the tack room.

"You should wear it at O'Roarke's," she called after him.

"Not happening," he shouted back. He deposited his saddle quickly and hurried back to grab hers before she tried to carry it herself. He arrived just in time. "Let me get that."

She opened her mouth as if to protest.

"Please. I like showing off my cowboy-ish skills."

"Okay." She grinned and stepped away from the horse. "Sure you won't wear the hat at the brewhouse? The customers would love it."

"Not doing it." He piled the cinch and the stirrups on top of the saddle.

"Then will you promise to wear it when we have outdoor sex?"

He picked up the saddle and turned back toward her. "As I suspected, it had nothing to do with keeping the sun out of your eyes, did it?"

"Not really. Sex with you is always great, but when you wear that hat…" She sighed and patted her chest.

"Then I'd better not wear it at O'Roarke's." He carried the saddle into the barn. "I'm liable to be mobbed."

"Good point. Save it for when you're with me."

He came back out with the plastic tote that held the grooming tools and smiled at her. "That I can do." And now he had a reason to take the hat to Seattle.

"Are you going to brush them down?"

"I am."

"Let me help. We used to brush the horses at the stable where I rode."

"By all means."

"Yay!" She picked up a brush and started in on Isabeau.

He watched her for a minute before turning back to Navarre. Yep, life was perfect right now. Caring for the horses together after going for a ride and making love ranked high on his list of favorite ways to spend a morning. He wondered if he'd have trouble getting back into his regular routine.

Once the horses were turned out into the pasture, Chelsea wanted to go back to the cabin to check the Kickstarter site. A few small donations had come in, so they were inching closer. They only had two days left, but now Damon and Cade could totally cover the rest if necessary.

"I just have a feeling something more has happened," she said.

"Go ahead and check." Finn gave her a quick kiss. "I'll see if Rosie needs any help with lunch." It would only be the four of them today. Damon and Phil were at the lumber yard and planned to stay in town for lunch. Cade was with Lexi looking at a horse she was considering buying.

When Finn walked into the kitchen, Rosie had the refrigerator door open and was pulling sandwich fixings out of the refrigerator.

"Just in time." She handed him a loaf of bread. "Enjoy your ride?"

"We did." He was glad she still had her back to him because she'd surely guessed what had happened during that ride. "Thanks for loaning us Navarre and Isabeau."

"Anytime. Herb and I don't ride them as much as we

should." She gave him several packages of lunch meat. "Where's Chelsea?"

"Checking on Kickstarter."

"I looked early this morning and we'd gained another twenty-five bucks. Every little bit helps." She took out mustard and mayonnaise and some lettuce before closing the door with her hip. "Herb's catching up on his email. He'll probably look again before he shuts down the computer."

"Chelsea had a hunch more had happened this morning. Maybe we're over the top and don't even know it." He washed up at the sink so he could help with the sandwiches.

"Wouldn't that be great?" Rosie took down a large breadboard that hung on the wall. "Cade, Lexi and Damon keep saying they'll cover what's left, but I'd rather they didn't have to."

"I know, but it's not much if they split it three ways, and missing by such a small amount would be stupid." He finished drying his hands and glanced over as Herb walked into the kitchen. "Hey, did you look at Kickstarter?"

Herb didn't say anything. Instead he glanced at Rosie and swallowed.

"Dad?" Herb's expression made Finn's stomach begin to churn.

About that time the front door banged and Chelsea raced into the kitchen, breathing hard. "A backer canceled." She gulped in air. "A really big one."

A chill settled over him as he stared at her, not wanting to believe what he'd heard but knowing it was true. Herb had seen it, too. He just hadn't figured out how to tell Rosie.

Rosie turned from the counter and gazed at Chelsea. "How bad is it?"

"I won't lie to you." Chelsea's face had drained of color. "It's bad. We'll start contacting people right away to see if we can raise more money, but…"

Rosie shook her head. "No. Everyone's been more than generous. All our friends, all our boys, even strangers we don't know. I'm not asking them to give more."

"I'll ask," Chelsea said. "You don't have to. I'll—"

"No. Thank you, but no." Rosie came over and put her hands on Chelsea's shoulders. "Even if you're the one asking, it's still like us asking. We have forty-eight hours left. Maybe something will happen. If not…we tried."

Finn recovered his voice. "Can someone do that? Just back out?"

"They can up until twenty-four hours before the deadline." Chelsea's gaze was bleak. "This is one of the ranchers who came to the presentation last Saturday. He sent me an email and he's devastated, but his wife had a sudden health crisis and insurance won't cover it. The bills will be enormous. He has no choice."

"Of course he doesn't." Rosie squeezed Chelsea's shoulders. "Here's my philosophy. If something is supposed to work out, it will. Now let's have some lunch."

The meal was a quiet one. Finn ate because it seemed impolite not to after the food had been prepared. He and Chelsea had planned to sand the benches that ringed the fire pit this afternoon. Because he had no better idea for how to fill the time, he suggested to Chelsea they go ahead and she agreed.

"But first I'll call Damon and Cade," he told Rosie as he, Herb and Chelsea helped clean up the lunch dishes.

"Let me call them," Rosie said. "I need to emphasize

to them what I just told all of you. We're going to stand pat and see what happens. No heroics."

He recognized the steely determination in her voice and knew there was no arguing with her. "All right."

As he and Chelsea walked back to the cabins, she didn't say anything. He was grateful for her silence. What was there to say?

Damon had designated the second cabin Construction Central, so that's where Finn and Chelsea went for the sandpaper blocks Damon had put together for them to use. The benches were old and he hadn't wanted to use a power sander.

They each picked a bench, straddled it and began to sand. The mindless work was perfect. He was too dazed to be good for much else. They'd worked steadily for almost an hour when his phone chirped. Probably Damon or Cade.

He checked the text ID. So his assistant Brad had decided to check in after being silent all week. Finn had been kind of relieved not to hear from the guy.

Climbing off the bench, he walked away from the fire pit. It had been an instinctive move, but he was aware of Chelsea watching him. He put the phone to his ear and kept his voice down. "Hey, Brad. What's up?"

"We have a situation here."

Of course they did. It figured that everything was turning to shit at once. But he doubted anything could be as bad as the news about Kickstarter. "What's that?"

"Jeff quit last night."

"Why?" Jeff was his most experienced bartender. He trained the new hires and was the steadiest employee Finn had.

"Crisis with his family back in New Jersey. I'm not

clear on the details but somebody has cancer and he's needed there."

"Don't let him quit. Give him a leave of absence."

"I tried that. He wouldn't go for it. Said he'd be relocating to Jersey, something about taking care of his little sister. He's not coming back, Finn."

"He's left already?" He felt the first prick of unease. Jeff was the wheelhorse of the waitstaff—bartenders, servers, the whole shebang.

"Yeah, and we need somebody with his level of experience. Roger's not ready to take over."

"No, he's not." Jeff had been training Roger to step in when he was on vacation, but the guy was too young to take over Jeff's position permanently.

"I have somebody in mind who might work out."

"Do I know him?"

"No. He's from Portland. But he has friends in Seattle and has been considering making a change."

Alarm bells went off in Finn's head. He'd done all the hiring from the first day. Sure, he'd made a couple of mistakes with the lower-paying positions, but he'd filled the important jobs with the right people.

Jeff had been one of those people, and now Brad was suggesting that they bring in some unknown from Portland, somebody Finn had never met. A bad hire at this point could have lasting repercussions.

He glanced at Chelsea, who was still watching him, and he wondered if she'd have any words of wisdom. But she didn't have employees. She couldn't understand how critical this was to the future of O'Roarke's. Jeff had a legion of admirers, and whoever took his place would need the same charisma.

It sounded as if this Portland guy might be a friend of Brad's. That wouldn't help Brad make an objective decision. Cronyism might be involved. Finn had to make the call. He hated what that would entail—leaving the ranch today if possible. But, seriously, what could he do here?

Chelsea probably wouldn't want to go and there was no reason she should have to pack up and leave. She could drive the SUV back to Jackson and fly out when they'd planned to.

He didn't like the idea of taking off right now, but Rosie had lectured him about not letting this project screw up his business. She'd been very clear.

"Invite your friend for an interview," he said, "but make it for tomorrow afternoon at the earliest. I want to be there."

"That's why I called you. I thought you might."

"I'll try to get a flight out today. I'll let you know."

"Great. Safe travels."

"Thanks." Finn disconnected. Then he turned to meet Chelsea's gaze. "There's a crisis at work."

"What sort of crisis?"

"Jeff, my most valuable bartender who kept everything running smoothly, has quit."

"Sorry to hear that."

"I have to fly out today."

She leaned on the bench and looked at him, her expression giving nothing away. She used to wear that expression a lot before this trip, but he hadn't seen it recently. "Today?"

"I have to go, Chels. Brad knows a guy from Portland, but this is too important a position to fill based on his friendship with Brad. I need to get a look at the guy. Résumés don't give the whole picture. I need to talk to him."

"You're not willing to take Brad's word that he's right for the job?"

"For any other position, sure. But this is too important to leave to chance. We're replacing a key employee."

"I understand the significance of that."

"Do you? Because you're a company of one. I'm not. Hiring the right people is critical to the success of the operation."

She put down her sandpaper block and got up from the bench. "I may be a company of one, as you phrase it, but I work with clients like you who have many employees. Jeff was an important component. Whenever I went into O'Roarke's and he was there, he lit up the place."

"So you do understand. I'm glad, because—"

"I understand that you feel the need to supervise the hiring of Jeff's replacement."

"Yes, ma'am, I do." He tugged down the brim of Cade's hat to make the point.

She didn't smile. In fact, disappointment dulled the usual sparkle in her brown eyes. "But I don't understand that you're willing to leave Thunder Mountain when the Kickstarter deadline is tomorrow night."

He felt as if he'd been slapped. "Chels, I have to sit in on that interview. I can't take a chance that Brad will hire the wrong person."

"Can't you?" Her voice was a soft plea. "Is that really more important than supporting the people you love while they sweat out this deadline?"

"My presence won't affect the damned contributions!"

"Of course not, but you can lend your moral support! Win or lose, they need you here."

"That makes no sense. Even Rosie said I shouldn't jeopardize my business for Thunder Mountain Academy. Yet you're telling me I should?"

She stared at him for several long, agonizing moments. "No, I'm not. It's your decision to make." And she walked away.

"Don't go. Talk to me, Chels."

She turned back and gazed at him. Her voice shook. "I didn't intend to say this yet, if ever, but I love you, Finn."

He gasped. She'd chosen to tell him now?

"And because I love you, I'm not going to ask you to change a pattern that is so deeply ingrained. You do what you think is best."

"But you don't think it's best, do you?" Now he felt as if someone had poured cement in his veins.

"What I think doesn't matter."

"It does matter." His whole body ached. "Please tell me. I want to know."

She sighed. "Okay. I realize that it's a significant position, but Brad is a capable assistant. You should be able to trust him to make this decision."

"It's not that simple."

"It's exactly that simple. If you can't trust your assistant to act in your absence on matters large and small, then you're locked into a situation where you'll have to supervise every detail forever. I love you, but I'm not willing to deal with that mindset. Your decision to leave now tells me that your thinking hasn't changed at all." She gazed at him. "We'd have no chance, Finn. We'd crash and burn." Tossing down the sanding block, she walked away.

And instead of going toward the cabin they'd shared, she headed up to the ranch house, as if making it clear that her loyalty was to Thunder Mountain Ranch and not him.

She really didn't get it, probably because her operation was so different from his. She couldn't see how a bad decision now had the potential for a domino effect. If the wrong person took over Jeff's position, gradually Finn's customer base would disappear. His revenues would drop off and he'd begin a slow slide into bankruptcy.

Good thing she hadn't gone back to the cabin, because he needed to boot up his laptop and make plane reservations. God, he felt stiff. He rolled his shoulders as he walked.

The minute he opened the door, he decided he'd have to take his laptop somewhere else. Chelsea wasn't physically there, but her presence could be felt as strongly as if she had been. There was her gray suitcase on the floor, and by now he knew every item in it.

They'd made the bed together this morning, just as they had every morning. He could see her plain as day, her hair mussed from sleep and good lovemaking as she dutifully helped him tug the covers into place, all the while complaining about having to get up before the chickens so they'd make it to breakfast on time.

This morning she'd started a pillow fight. He'd wanted to make love afterward, but they would have missed Rosie's breakfast. Being there had become a point of honor for both of them.

So he'd told himself it didn't matter because they'd be back in this bed tonight and eventually they'd be living together. They'd have plenty of pillow fights followed by great sex.

Apparently not.

He massaged the back of his neck where he'd developed a really bad crick. And he had the beginnings of a charley horse in his left calf. When he leaned down to pick up his laptop from the floor beside his suitcase, he felt a twinge in his lower back.

Damn it, now was not the time to be falling apart. He needed to be 100 percent to deal with the situation at

O'Roarke's. He left his hat inside and walked out to sit on the stoop with his laptop. Time to stop playing cowboy.

For some reason his fingers were clumsy on the keys and he blamed it on the sanding. That probably explained the pain in his shoulders and the crick in his neck, maybe even the charley horse. He'd been hunched over in an unnatural position for too long.

His stomach didn't feel all that great, either. He shouldn't have forced down that sandwich. And now the damned site was slow loading. He finally got something to come up, but all the flights he looked at for today, even the red-eye tonight, were booked. Sheridan didn't tend to have as many choices as a bigger city.

He decided to check other locations and found a red-eye leaving tonight out of Cheyenne. That wasn't optimal, but he might have to go with it. His neck really hurt. Straightening, he rubbed it some more as he looked around at the meadow and the three other cabins.

Except for the birds chirping in the nearby pine trees and the rustle of a slight breeze, the meadow was quiet. Peaceful. *Precious.* And not just to him. It was precious to his foster parents and all the boys who'd sat around the fire pit roasting marshmallows and singing silly camp songs.

This meadow had the potential to become precious to a whole new group of kids who would learn a lot about caring for horses and even more about how to live. They might even learn about potbellied pigs.

Hard to imagine that the fate of this meadow hung in the balance and would be decided tomorrow at midnight. He tried to convince himself to book his flight, but it wasn't a good option. Maybe he should take a break and try again in a few minutes. Things could change.

Shutting down the laptop, he left it on the stoop and

got to his feet. Slowly he walked around the fire pit until he came to the Brotherhood cabin. It was unlocked, so he walked inside, leaving the door open so he could hear the birds and the wind in the trees.

After all these years it still smelled the same. He closed his eyes and imagined being here at fifteen, before he'd kissed a girl, before he'd had a driver's license. He pictured what it had looked like with posters tacked on the walls. A radio was usually on because they'd all loved their music.

Cade's junk would be strewed around, but his and Damon's areas would be neat. Unless he was studying, his books, including *Charlotte's Web*, were always lined up on the shelf. He knew that book by heart, all the text and the illustrations.

Charlotte had stuck by that pig. When it looked as if nothing would save Wilbur, she'd stepped in. She'd been a true friend, a loyal friend. She hadn't abandoned him at the zero hour.

Opening his eyes, he rubbed a hand over his face. It came away wet. Slowly he turned around, reached up and traced the TMB initials he and his brothers had carved into the beam over the doorway. He thought of the pledge they'd recited during the blood brother ceremony. *Loyalty above all.*

When he heard footsteps in the grass, he immediately knew whose they were. He recognized them now.

Chelsea walked over and peered up at him. "Rosie sent me to ask if you need a ride to the airport. And, don't worry. I explained how important this is to you and she's fine with it."

"I'm not." His throat was clogged and the words came out sounding weird.

She came up the steps and stood just outside the door.

"Can't you get a flight? I figured it wouldn't be easy, but I was hoping, for your sake, that—"

"I'm not going."

Her stoic expression softened and emotion flickered in her gaze. "Why?"

"Because if it weren't for Rosie and Herb, and Cade and Damon, I wouldn't have a business. I might not even have a life. I owe them…" He paused, struggling to keep from breaking down.

"Oh, Finn." She came to him, wrapped him in her arms and buried her face against his chest. She was trembling.

He closed her in a tight embrace and laid his cheek against her soft hair. In that moment he regained his soul.

"I was so scared I'd lost you." Her voice was muffled against his shirt.

"Me, too. Literally petrified. All my muscles started locking up." He kissed the top of her head and stroked her hair.

"Wow." She lifted her head and her brown eyes were shining. "Epic."

"Yeah." He took his time looking into her eyes, because he would never again take that privilege for granted. "I love you, Chels, and not just because you're funny and sexy and beautiful and creative, even though you're all those things. I love you because you had the courage to tell me the truth, even when I didn't want to hear it."

She swallowed. "It wasn't easy."

"I know, and I hope to God I never again get that close to betraying everything and everyone I care about. But if I do…"

"I'll kick your butt." Her smile was filled with tenderness. "But I have a feeling you don't have to worry."

"I have a feeling you're right." When he kissed her, he swore he'd never take that privilege for granted, either. He'd come so close to ruining everything. But thanks to the inspiration of a tiny spider, a blood oath in the forest and the woman in his arms, he'd gained the world.

Epilogue

FINN'S DECISION TO STAY changed everything in Chelsea's mind. She was no longer worried about having him move in, and she was convinced that a miracle would happen and the Kickstarter campaign would be funded by the deadline. Logically his presence shouldn't have any effect, but she had a superstitious streak.

She could tell everyone else appreciated him being there, too, although she and Rosie were the only ones who knew how close he'd come to leaving. They'd both decided that talking about it after the fact would serve no purpose.

But despite Chelsea's firm belief that the money would appear, at one hour before the midnight deadline they were still short the amount that had dropped out yesterday, too much even for them all to cover.

Everyone had gathered in the kitchen where they had three different laptops on. Rosie plied everyone with snacks and free-flowing beer, all except for Chelsea and Rosie, who drank coffee and Bailey's.

At eleven-thirty, Ty Slater, a former foster kid and their legal consultant who lived in Cheyenne, showed up at the front door. When he walked into the kitchen,

Chelsea recognized him immediately from the calendar. Because it was a sixteen-month calendar, Ty had volunteered to be the cowboy on the page for September through December. Not even Cade had wanted to be hanging on someone's wall for that long.

But Ty apparently was willing to do anything he could to help the cause, including donating his legal services. "I was watching on my computer at home," he said, "and finally I couldn't stand it. I knew you'd all be sitting around hyperventilating, so I'm here to hyperventilate with you."

"And drink Finn's beer." Cade handed him a chilled bottle. "We planned to save some for when we reached the goal, but we decided to drink it now because we need to fortify ourselves."

"I understand. Tense times always call for a good beer." Ty pushed his brown Stetson to the back of his head and smiled at Chelsea. "Here's to you, lady. That was another reason to drive up, so I could meet our Kickstarter guru. You're amazing."

"She is amazing." Finn stepped up quietly behind her chair and put a hand on her shoulder. "I'm a lucky guy."

"I'd say so." Chelsea noticed Ty and Finn share a look, and the subtle flirting stopped immediately. "When are you two heading back to Seattle?"

"Tomorrow," Chelsea said. "It'll be tough to leave, though. I've loved being here."

"I'll bet. What kind of stuff did you do?"

"Helped Cade and Damon," Finn said, "but I had some time to show her around the place. One night we went dancing in town."

Ty blinked. "You? Dancing?"

"You'd be flabbergasted." Damon wandered over to

join the conversation. "Old Finn, the guy with two left feet, has found his rhythm. Now he puts me to shame."

"That I'd like to see." Ty peered at Finn. "What'd you do, take lessons?"

Finn laughed. "You might say that. Actually, I—"

"Oh, my God!" Chelsea had been keeping an eye on the screen off and on while she tried not to panic. Then she looked and...

"We're over!" Lexi jumped up from the table and grabbed Cade around the neck. "Somebody just donated a whole bunch, and we're over!"

The room erupted into cheers, shouts and a few quiet tears from Rosie. Chelsea thought she might have been the only one to see that because Rosie quickly wiped them away and began hugging everyone. Chelsea almost didn't hear her phone when it rang, even though it was right in her pocket.

"Who was the donor?" Ty asked.

"You check." Chelsea pulled out her phone and hurried into the living room where she could hear. "Lily? Did you see that we made it?"

"Duh. I just donated. I thought you guys were solid when you left here, but then I looked just now and you were seriously under, so I gave you the rest."

"What? But you already gave us a donation, Lily. I hate for you to go into debt. I'm grateful, but that's a chunk of money. And now you're stuck."

Finn had followed her into the living room and stood listening to her end of the conversation.

"I have plenty of money," Lily said. "Didn't anyone tell you? I made a killing on a video game a few years ago and I'm living off the royalties. I didn't want to be obnoxious and just throw money at you before. Then it would have been all about me."

"You could never be obnoxious, and thank God this didn't put you in the hole."

"Not even close to the hole."

"That's great to hear. Whew."

"Congratulations! Thunder Mountain Academy is a go!"

Chelsea took another deep breath and let the tension flow out of her body. "Yes, because of people like you."

"Hey, it took everybody to make this happen."

Chelsea paused to catch her breath. "And FYI, I may have Rosie talked into getting a pig. We're going to slow-play it, but be ready if the subject comes up."

"I will! Now go on back to the party. I'm sure there is one."

"There is. Good night, Lily." Chelsea disconnected the call and stared at Finn. "I think she's a millionaire or something. Who knew?"

"I don't think she wants the whole world to know." He pulled her into his arms. "Congratulations, Chels. This is mostly your victory, and I want you to go back in there and claim it, but—"

"Come here, cowboy." She pulled him by his shirtfront the way she had their first night in the Bunk and Grub.

"I love it when you do that."

"I'm glad, because I intend to be doing it for a long, long time."

"Then it looks like I'll be doing this for a long, long time." His mouth came down on hers.

Not surprisingly, his kiss was ended soon after it began. Cade and Damon broke it up and hauled them both back into the kitchen for a loud and jubilant toast.

But that was okay. Toasting the future of Thunder Mountain Academy was important. She'd have plenty of time for kissing once they returned to Seattle. And now, because Finn had seen the light, so would he.

* * * * *

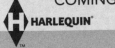

Available August 18, 2015

#859 A SEAL'S TEMPTATION
Uniformly Hot!
by Tawny Weber
Lark Sommers is too busy guarding her independence to admit she needs love. Navy SEAL Shane O'Brian is too busy protecting others to realize he yearns for a woman's touch. But the passion between them is about to ignite!

#860 ONE BREATHLESS NIGHT
Three Wicked Nights
by Jo Leigh
On New Year's Eve Rick Sinclair looks like danger and sex wrapped in a tux. Already engaged teacher Jenna Delaney is about to find out if he can teach *her* a few things.

#861 THIS KISS
Made in Montana
by Debbi Rawlins
Ethan Styles is the hottest bull rider on the circuit, but he doesn't stand a chance against one very sexy bounty hunter determined to give him the ride of his life!

#862 INSATIABLE
Unrated!
by Leslie Kelly
A favor from a handsome stranger turns into an insatiable affair that Viv Callahan doesn't want to end. Until she discovers that Damian Black is a tycoon...and that's not his only secret.

REQUEST YOUR FREE BOOKS!
2 FREE NOVELS PLUS 2 FREE GIFTS!

HARLEQUIN®

Blaze

red-hot reads!

YES! Please send me 2 FREE Harlequin® Blaze® novels and my 2 FREE gifts (gifts are worth about \$10). After receiving them, if I don't wish to receive any more books, I can return the shipping statement marked "cancel." If I don't cancel, I will receive 4 brand-new novels every month and be billed just \$4.74 per book in the U.S. or \$5.21 per book in Canada. That's a savings of at least 14% off the cover price. It's quite a bargain. Shipping and handling is just 50¢ per book in the U.S. and 75¢ per book in Canada.* I understand that accepting the 2 free books and gifts places me under no obligation to buy anything. I can always return a shipment and cancel at any time. Even if I never buy another book, the two free books and gifts are mine to keep forever.

150/350 HDN GH2D

Name	(PLEASE PRINT)

Address		Apt. #

City	State/Prov.	Zip/Postal Code

Signature (if under 18, a parent or guardian must sign)

Mail to the **Reader Service:**
IN U.S.A.: P.O. Box 1867, Buffalo, NY 14240-1867
IN CANADA: P.O. Box 609, Fort Erie, Ontario L2A 5X3

Want to try two free books from another line?
Call 1-800-873-8635 or visit www.ReaderService.com.

"I can do almost anything with clay. Pottery is my passion, but I really enjoy sculpting, too. Hang on." Lark smiled and held up one finger, as if Shane would leave the minute she turned around.

She swept into the storage room and bent low to get something from the bottom shelf. And Shane knew it'd take an explosion to get him to move.

Because that was one sweet view.

He watched the way the fabric of her dress sort of floated over what looked to be a Grade A ass, then had to shove his hands into his pockets to hide his reaction.

As Lark came back with something in her hand, she gave him a smile that carried a hint of embarrassment, but unless she could read his mind, he didn't know what she had to be embarrassed about.

"You might like this," she said quietly, wetting her lips before holding out her hand, palm up.

On it was a small, whimsical dragon. Wings unfurled, it looked as if it was smiling.

"You made this?" Awed at the way the colors bled from red to gold to purple, he rubbed one finger over the tiny, detailed scales of the dragon's back. "It's great."

"He's a guardian dragon," Lark said, touching her finger to the cool ceramic, close enough that all he'd have to do was shift his hand to touch her. "You might like one of your own. I can tell Sara worries about you."

Shane grimaced at the idea of his baby sister telling people—especially sexy female people with eyes like midnight—that he needed protecting. Better to change the subject than comment on that.

"It takes a lot of talent to make something this intricate," he said, waiting until her gaze met his to slide his hand over hers. He felt her fingers tremble even as he saw that spark heat. Her lips looked so soft as she puffed out a soft breath before tugging that full bottom cushion between her teeth. He wanted to do that for her, just nibble there for a little while.

"I'm good with my hands," she finally said, her words so low they were almost a whisper.

How good? he wanted to ask, just before he dared her to prove it.

Don't miss
A SEAL'S TEMPTATION by Tawny Weber.
Available in September 2015 wherever
Harlequin® Blaze® books and ebooks are sold.

www.Harlequin.com

HARLEQUIN®

A *Romance* FOR EVERY MOOD™

JUST CAN'T GET ENOUGH?

Join our social communities
and talk to us online.

You will have access to the latest
news on upcoming titles and special
promotions, but most importantly,
you can talk to other fans about your
favorite Harlequin reads.

Harlequin.com/Community

 Facebook.com/HarlequinBooks

Twitter.com/HarlequinBooks

 Pinterest.com/HarlequinBooks

HARLEQUIN®

A *Romance* FOR EVERY MOOD™

**Stay up-to-date on all your
romance-reading news with the
Harlequin Shopping Guide,
featuring bestselling authors, exciting new
miniseries, books to watch and more!**

The newest issue will be delivered right to you
with our compliments! There are 4 each year.

Signing up is easy.

EMAIL

ShoppingGuide@Harlequin.ca

WRITE TO US

HARLEQUIN BOOKS
Attention: Customer Service Department
P.O. Box 9057, Buffalo, NY 14269-9057

OR PHONE

1-800-873-8635 in the United States
1-888-343-9777 in Canada

Please allow 4-6 weeks for delivery of the first issue by mail.